Dedication

This collection of short stories is dedicated to Dave 'Daisy' Ratcliffe,
An honest, funny, and decent bloke.
1946 - 2011

Deadly Sins
First published in Australia by Ian Laver 2024
Copyright © Ian Laver 2024
All Rights Reserved

 A catalogue record for this
book is available from the
National Library of Australia

ISBN: 978-0-6451887-4-5 (pbk)
ISBN: 978-0-6451887-5-2 (ebk)

Cover design by Jan Forbes © 2024

Typesetting and design by Publicious Book Publishing
Published in collaboration with Publicious Book Publishing
www.publicious.com.au

Disclaimer
These stories are works of fiction. All characters are fictious and any resemblance to actual persons, living or dead is entirely coincidental. Some geographical locations exist but some are invented.

Foreword

So, who is Ian Laver? Tricky question: the answer depends on who is asking. He is a well-loved local writer and storyteller, an active community worker, an international traveller, and more. But the Ian I know best is a woodsmith and a wordsmith. As a woodsmith, he takes rough pieces of timber and fashions these into unique, beautifully crafted pieces of furniture. And as a wordsmith, he takes rough slices of life, and fashions these into unique, beautifully crafted stories. Ian brings his gentle philosophy of life, his considerable talent, and his broad life experience to both pursuits, and especially to his writing.

In this collection, Ian has gathered some of his earlier stories, with diverse characters and themes - stories that will have you doubled over with laughter, and yet will unexpectedly touch your heart. His keen eye for quirky characters, his quick ear for Aussie dialogue, and his fine sense of the ridiculous come together in these engaging stories.

Reader, beware! To pick up this book is to give yourself over to laughter, to new horizons of the unexpected, to the pleasure of meeting new characters. Like his fine furniture, Ian's stories will intrigue you and leave you eager for more, more, more.

Bronwyn Cozens
Doctor of Creative Writing

Author's note

Deadly Sins is a collection of my early short stories, mostly written from prompts whilst in writers' groups. Prompts dictated certain criteria; to be seen through the eyes of a child; or for a character to get away with a crime - or be caught; or be seen from a given point of view; or to contain humour, wanton violence, or a given emotion; and so on.

This collection offers diverse characters and sins; some characters are dark, cruel, criminal and others innocent, brave, youthful. There are also characters from the varied layers of society; the rich, spoilt, privileged and the born to lose, as well as those, who despite the odds, can overcome adversity.

There are many great Australian writers, too many to list, who have led the way, and influenced my desire to write. Australians have a unique perspective on life and some of this is reflected in my stories.

There are five American writers, Larry McMurtry, Cormac McCarthy, Charles Bukowski, Jim Thompson, and Michael Connelly who have also influenced me.

The stories in *Deadly Sins* are diverse and I hope you will enjoy reading them and meeting some of the characters.

Ian

DEADLY SINS

CONTENTS

The path of life

Is sometimes harsh

Grasp an opportunity when presented

BREAK

"Bastards," mumbled Shorty stooping to walk through the doorway. He looked at his father lying on the bed, tubes sticking out in every direction. Antiseptic and the whiff of bed pan hung in the air. Shorty wondered how they could afford to give their dad the medical treatment needed.

He stepped aside to allow a bed to squelch by on rubber wheels. A frantic nurse waved and yelled. Shorty's eyes prickled. *That could be dad if he doesn't have a lung transplant.*

The waiting area boiled with humanity, mainly the sick. Country hospitals were the same as city hospitals, always busy. Shorty shouldered his way through the crowd, ears trying to blot out sharp announcements from a loudspeaker system that could have been borrowed from sideshow alley.

Dad gave 35 years to Hilltop Mining, those bastards. As far as he was concerned the management knew about the dangers of asbestos way back, 40 or 50 years ago. Now, as the old workers became ill, the company easily dodged the claims with their slick lawyers. He knew that was the way business was done these days. Sell out or go bankrupt, change the name of the company, and start up all over again. How was he going to generate the money for his dad's operation? They would have to go to the city and there were huge costs associated with surgeons and hospital, as well as ongoing medical fees and drugs.

Shorty drove in the direction of home, deep in thought. As he rounded a bend on the lonely road, an emergency scene jerked him to his senses. A late model BMW car had crashed against a tree on the other side of the road. Heart in mouth, he leapt out and ran over to the hot wreck, his Rural Fire Service training clicked in. Lively talkback radio bubbled away in the background. A hissing sound and a small amount of steam rose from around the bonnet. He knew the accident had just happened. The windscreen and part of the front pillar was caved in. The driver's head had been crushed. Shorty quickly checked for a pulse with trembling fingers, sweat trickling down his face. The man was obviously dead, he could not perform CPR anyway because the body was jammed against the steering wheel.

It was then he noticed the man's wallet. He picked it up and flipped it open with the thought that having a name to give police and ambulance would be helpful. His temples began to pulse.

"Bloody hell," he gasped, "it can't be."

Shorty knew the name, Denzel Kennedy, chief executive officer, Hilltop Mining. As he leant across to turn off the radio something on the passenger's side floor caught his eye. He reached over and pulled out the bag. Inside were six wads, at least two inches thick, of used $50 and $100 notes. Shorty looked up at the sky for a moment. Decision made. He wiped the radio dial and door handle, carefully wiped the wallet which he tossed on the floor and walked quickly back to his car.

Shorty slipped the bag under the seat and grabbed his mobile. Sweat dripped from his forehead as he dialled 000.

The end

Focus on the job

Keep desire in check

Other agendas abound

DRINK UP

Clinton nudged the solid teak door with his hip and dropped the key on the bureau. He turned the air-conditioning unit on full and flicked his shoes off on the way to the mini bar.

"Just as well the boss is paying," he mumbled, grabbing a can of Kingfisher, India's favourite beer. "Ahhh, that's better." Two more guzzles finished the can and he crushed it. He burped loudly and pulled out another.

He opened the safe and deposited a few valuables. Clinton collapsed his tired bulk onto the king-size bed and lay spreadeagled. The air-conditioning unit whirred away at the sticky heat.

"Blow it all," he said in the direction of the tiny private balcony at the Hotel Diamond.

Rain spat and speckled the glass as one of India's monsoonal storms dictated outdoor activities for the afternoon. The room pretended to be a little cooler but it did nothing to improve his mood. Wasting most of yesterday standing in front of the airport, all the smells - diesel, dogs, dust, shit, and piss - and the heat, as well as touts climbing all over him trying to give special prices for everything on earth. Waiting for Raju who got the times mixed up. Next came a bastard of a taxi ride with a dick-head driver who turned up the Bollywood bellow of frantic baby voice whine on the radio.

Then followed a hassle with the boy who was no boy. Little mongrel wanted a hundred rupees just to carry his bags to the room.

3

Most of the remaining part of the day with Raju was just like trying to organise school children. All the time sweat soaked his clothes as he dealt with people who had no bloody idea. He rubbed his forehead; in this country no one seemed to agree on anything. He had to admit Raju was doing his best but it was exactly the same as his last visit to Puttabad, problem after problem after problem. Clinton managed a small smile because everyone in India said, *no problem, no problem*, all the time. He looked out at the low grey battleship clouds.

The rain created a waterfall from the parapet above the outside balcony. Every few minutes a greater gush of water picked up flashing lights from the Hotel sign way above and presented a string of diamonds. He wondered if the owners had seen the same thing and had named the hotel appropriately. He doubted it. The whole water thing was fascinating and beautiful but he still felt like Tony Hancock on a wet Sunday afternoon. The boredom made him think it was time to do something else with his life. Six years of India. It had been okay for a while, an adventure. He would be thirty-eight soon, time to move into some other area of expertise. The messing about far outweighed the excitement.

The Diamond was the best hotel in town, but there was still a faint far off whiff of mould or mildew. Every hotel in India he had ever stayed in had that signature, from the absolute best, a grand a night to the dregs at ten bucks a night. It seemed to him the jungle signalling it was forever ready to grow back in. Vines in the street crept and strangled the median strips as well as trying to pull down the walls of the houses. Thorny acacias waited in the wings, forever gathering dusty rubbish strewn earth. In the front of this international hotel weeds prised the broken pavement apart, even on the main footpath. He thought India needed a billion people or more, and almost as many other animals, just to keep the jungle at bay.

Clinton rolled his muscled frame off the bed, padded to the mini bar, examined the options, and selected a can of gin and tonic. He zipped the lid off and guzzled. Drink in one hand he grabbed the towel off the bed and went into the bathroom. He fiddled with the complicated tap system, smiled at the complementary shower cap, and stepped under the cold shower. Clinton thought he heard a knock but it sounded like next door. He slowly dried himself, looking in the mirror, frowning at the jetlag bags under his eyes. He stood up to his six foot two, sucked his stomach in and flexed his bicep making the tattoo leap. He vigorously rubbed some conditioner through close cropped brown hair with practiced hands. There was that knock again. He had not ordered room service. Wrapping the towel around his waist he ambled out of the bathroom.

A rustle of silk. A woman stepped into the room and clicked the ancient heavy wooden door. Her eyes widened. She shook her magnificent shiny black mane.

"Oh! Oh! I am so sorry. What are you doing here? This is my room. Umm… I think."

To Clinton the words danced beautifully in the way Indian women speak. They stared; mild shock delayed a response.

"Umm, no, sorry. It can't be your room, the room was locked and I used my key, see, on the dresser, over there, room 252."

"Oh. I am so sorry, I … I have my floors mixed up; I think. The key, mmm, the key, the tag on my key it is lost, that's right, my room must be 352."

They stood looking at each other for a moment. The rain had stopped, and distant vehicle air horns trumpeted through the polluted air of the city, penetrating the whirring air-conditioner. He wanted her to stay.

She continued, "All rooms look the same. The brass disc fell off somewhere and I forgot my number. I have been looking everywhere."

Clinton, wrapped in a towel, stood there. He could see the red dot in the middle of her forehead. The third eye.

"I am so sorry, think I had better go," she said with an awkward smile.

"No, don't go. Er … how about a drink?" He knew how lame it sounded. It prompted him to move towards the mini bar.

"I'd better go." She stood motionless, except for the slight rise and fall of her breasts below an intricate tassel silver necklace.

He tried to think of a reason. "Why?"

"This is not … umm, how are you saying it, appropriate?"

"Oh, yes of course. How about a drink, later? At the Red Fort Lounge?"

They stared at each other.

"Yes, maybe." She shook her magnificent hair. It went down to a slim silver-belted waist.

She moved a hand behind and opened the door. The light from the passageway shone straight through her sari highlighting male-magnet curves. She spun on bare feet. There was a faint tinkle from petite silver bells around her ankles and a delicate swish of silk. She glanced over her shoulder. Her penetrating eyes found him again.

"Bye bye," she breathed and clicked the door.

Clinton stood still for several moments and then went over to touch the door handle. It was human warm. He could smell the faintest frangipani. No dream.

The next few hours disappeared with Clinton perched on the edge of the bed doing his best to clean up the mini-bar. The storm had gone, one empty bottle and two beer cans in time.

He grabbed clean, casual clothes with the idea he would go and check for any messages at the front desk and then have a drink in the Red Fort Lounge. The thought that a Hindu princess might appear was very much a long shot but he smiled at himself in the mirror on the way out.

"Yes sir, Mr Clinton, of course, from Mr Raju, sir. He will be collecting you at eight thirty in the morning," said the friendly young man at the front counter. He wore the usual hotel uniform - white body shirt, dark tie and black trousers.

"By the way, Yougesh," enquired Clinton squinting at the name tag on his pocket. "Would you be kind enough to tell me who is in room 352?"

"Room 352?" the young man moved his head in the smooth, friendly Indian fashion, "I think you are being mistaken, sir. Our rooms only go to 340."

Clinton's brain stopped. He did not hear the next sentence.

"... but we have plans to build another 60 rooms later this year, sir ..."

However, his analytical mind clicked in as he heard …

"… and please by the way sir be making sure that you are locking your room and using the safe facilities provided. There have been reports of theft from two of our rooms much to the embarrassment of this hotel, sir. Our security staffs are looking for a young Hindu woman, someone from outside. The hotel is most internally secure now, sir. There is no need to be alarmed at all, sir; everything is well in the hand." An Indian family arrived. "Will that be all Mr Clinton, sir? Excuse me, please."

Clinton did not hear Kenny Gee playing softly on the piped music system, nor did he recall walking into the lounge.

"Hello? Hi!"

He turned. He did not recognize her at first. She stood holding something up, jangling between thumb and forefinger. She was dressed in the western way but there was still a prominent red dot on her forehead.

"I found it!" Her smile was electric. "On the floor in my room."

Clinton stared at the key ring with the brass tag.

"See? The reception, Yougesh, my young friend, how are you saying it … crimpled the tag back on to the key ring? See? Room number 332, not 352." She shook her long shiny black hair, a slow billowing wave.

His smile masked enormous relief as well as the effect of her quaint musical use of English. He could not stop himself from helping. "Umm, I think the word is crimped."

"Yes, of course." Her kohl painted gaze lowered. "I feel so silly, startling you like that in your room. "My name is Sumitra." She held out a hand, red fingernails, several rings, no wedding band. A selection of brightly coloured bangles slid from her elbow to her wrist in the action.

"Steve, Steve Clinton." He smiled and took her hand which was offered in the gentle soft greeting favoured by Indians. He was not sure whether he hung on too long or whether she did.

"Oh, last names are so unnecessary, don't you think?" She laughed; eyes trapped him again. White healthy teeth hid behind moist bright red lips.

He smiled. "I'll tell you a story in a moment, but let's have a drink; it looks like you've just finished yours, anyway." He nodded towards her empty glass, needing a second or two to anchor himself.

"I love stories. A gin and tonic, please." She gently stroked some forward falling strands of hair behind her ears. Two silver earrings swayed.

The turbaned waiter was half way over to their table.

"Two gin and tonics, please, and some … peanuts?" He looked towards her. She nodded. Piped hotel music melded with the faint sounds of love and hardship beyond the walls out there in India.

"Now, Steve. Your story?" Her eyes flashed.

Clinton related what Yougesh said. He did not mention he had thought it was her.

"Mmm." She gazed at him hard. "I hope you didn't think that woman was me?"

He tried to hold her stare; he was good at it most of the time. "No, of course not."

She continued looking, then eased a slow smile and lifted her eyes. "Ah, our drinks are here."

Clinton was thankful a greater being let him off the hook.

He responded. "Here's cheers," to take his mind off looking at her low-cut dress and silver necklace. It was obvious she wore no bra.

They clinked glasses and eased back into the plush seats. Her light floral cotton skirt rose slightly above the knee when she crossed one slim brown leg over the other. The tiny silver ankle bracelet tinkled above her silver braid high heels. He knew she knew he was looking.

Her mobile rang. "Excuse me, you don't mind …?"

"No, of course not, please go ahead."

She picked up the phone and clicked heels towards the door. His eyes were drawn to her exquisite figure accentuated by patio lights behind. Clinton was sure there was nothing much underneath. He could not believe all of this was happening. The situation had gone from a meeting with the beautiful woman in unusual circumstances, then believing she was a thief, and then realising she was not. And then, after all that, he was almost convinced she liked him.

"Work," she offered, gracefully sitting down again. "I am in the travel business. I move around quite a bit checking out accommodation, conference venues and dining facilities for corporate people. What do you do, Steve?" She lowered her head slightly, fixing him again with her penetrating dark eyes.

"I'm in the homewares industry. I come to India with designs and find people to make bedspreads, tablecloths, cushion covers, curtains, blinds, that sort of thing." Clinton was eager to get off that well used subject. He ordered another round of drinks and asked her questions about work.

At the point where he was wondering how to ask her to dinner, she said, "Maybe we should go to dinner, yes?"

Dinner under the soft lights of Shah Jahan's Restaurant drifted until late in the evening. Sumitra took care of their ordering and many wonderful Indian dishes arrived at the table. The fine array of sumptuous food was helped along with several bottles of expensive red wine. When the bill arrived at the table, she held her hand out towards the chit.

Clinton shook his head, "No, allow me, I insist. I have an expense account." He was cruising along drunk enough, and figured she was as well. He found it easy to say, "Would you like to come back to my room for a nightcap?"

She gave a throaty laugh that excited him. "I shouldn't really. I have a busy day tomorrow."

"Just one, I have some good quality duty-free whisky. There's never any harm in the one."

She looked at him a long moment, and then he felt her touch his calf with a toe. Shoes did not feel like that. "Umm, one only? Promise?"

"Of course. Unless you want more."

She laughed her throaty laugh again, huskier this time, and slipped her arm through his, nudging his upper thigh gently with her hip as they swayed out towards the lifts.

He fiddled with the key and eventually the heavy door unlocked.

"Please, have a seat."

She kicked her shoes off and sat on the bed near the pillows. He stumbled to the bureau, grabbed two glasses, and with fumbling fingers opened the whiskey.

"Ice?"

"No, straight please." She leant back against the pillows and her dress rode high up on her thighs. "Just one." She laughed again, taking the glass.

He lurched over, gulped his, clattered his empty glass alongside hers on the bedside table and slumped down alongside her. He fanned his fingers into her hair, and drew her face towards him, already entranced and lost in her beauty.

∞

Bells rang through what seemed like a metre of mud. Flashing daylight clawed at his eyes. Harsh bells jangled in his brain. No, it was the phone. Clinton tried to move his head, could not, it was full of gravel and sharp things.

It took several rings before he realised where he was. His clumsy hands felt like he had welders' gloves on. After several attempts he found the receiver.

A strange noise, like someone talking from under the sea. "Sir, this is Yougesh here, sir, from the front desk. Mr Raju, he is waiting for you to see you, sir."

Clinton's brain searched. His mouth tried to speak. It did not work. He tried again. "Okay." It sounded like bouquet.

"Er ... Mr Clinton, sir, is everything being all right?"

Clinton shook his head. It hurt. His mouth felt thick. "I'll be down soon, thank you."

It did not sound normal. He somehow found the phone cradle after a couple of tries. He drew himself to a sitting position, massaging his head, trying to focus on something. Standing up proved a problem, he stumbled and grabbed the wardrobe door. The first thing he noticed was the tell-tale gaping cave of the safe.

"No, no!" he tried to say. It felt like someone had poked a white-hot knitting needle into his ear.

The huge wad of Australian dollars to bribe people in the sting was gone. Grease money. Gone. His wallet with all the local money and credit cards. Gone. His identification papers and passport. Gone. He fossicked through the cupboard but he knew the Jet-flash was missing. It contained a detailed list of Australian nationals of Indian descent who were terrorist suspects.

"No!" he said again softly but the pain was acute and it felt like blood and acid was oozing out of his ears. But it was worse; he knew it, much worse, if it was possible to be so. His firearm was gone. All the problems associated with bringing a firearm into India, all the paperwork, the accountability forms. How in the hell was he going to explain this, not only to the boss back in Australia, but to Agent Raju of the Indian Special Anti-Terrorist Unit?

Clinton, seconded to assist the ISATU by ASIO, crumpled to the floor. Thoughts slowly clawed back through the fog in painful jabs. He tried to remember details about last night, busying himself as he signed the bill, she handed him his glass. *Drink up, Steve*, she said. He could hear her beautiful honey voice, *Drink up, Steve*. Those beautiful dark eyes.

He glanced up and saw that the duty-free whisky was also gone. He also realised that he was still fully clothed.

Inspector Steve Clinton held his head, convulsed forward, and vomited.

The end

Spin a yarn

Same as a lie

Bullies always rule

SPINNERS

The Conservative Prime Minister leant back; hands clasped behind his head. The opulent office chair sighed. He was more than pleased the direction things were going with the looming election. His sultans of spin had really cranked up the positive aspects of the government's high points over the last three years. But, more than that, they had hammered home the inadequacies of the opposition, who only a week ago had looked more than reasonably good.

The Deputy Prime Minister, Norman Everidge, crossed one leg over the other. His razor-sharp creases kept their vigil. "Yes, Sir Reuben, we are in a much stronger position than we were before the last election."

The Prime Minister, Sir Reuben Miller-Anderson, had managed to snaffle a knighthood for his service to the Crown. The left saw it as a service to big business and banks. He was aware, however, that others did not give a root because they had stocks and shares, rental properties, and there was, of course, the great slovenly army who did not vote. His government had been in for a record four terms. Big hands slid around the gold embossed leather blotter. The chair gave a ping.

"Damned right, Norm, not only have our spinners made us sound good by giving money to private schools, they made that doomed contract with the Yanks for those obsolete jet fighters sound like a real bargain. How the hell they do it, when a couple of weeks ago it was clear that we had been ripped off blind. I mean, how could old Tugboat, our good old scholar defence bloody minister, have signed the deal when we wouldn't get the ignition switches until three years after delivery?"

Norm smiled, "Yeah, bloody Tugger downed too many scotches that afternoon at the American Embassy, although it would have been bourbon knowing him. He's going a bit overboard, Reuben, admittedly the kickbacks we got were pretty good but the bastard's too careless these days, we'll have to give him an ambassador post after the election."

Sir Reuben nodded and chuckled. "Fancy our spinners making our bid to give pensioners and single parents that extra $220 a year seem a generous benefit; even a dim-wit could see we get $250 back! Hell, those fellers are good. I mean, the Shadow Treasurer had offered carers and the disabled a much better deal and our spinners made *them* look like liars."

"No doubt about it Prime Minister I wouldn't go so far as to say we couldn't lose, but ..." Norm was buoyant; a win would mean a knighthood for him as well.

The Prime Minister opened a drawer and pulled out two tumblers; a hand went down and a bottle of 35-year-old Chivas Regal Premium Scotch Whisky appeared from his bottom drawer.

"Who needs ice?" laughed Sir Reuben.

The clink was Swedish lead crystal or better.

∞

"Bloody hell!" barked Doug Wright as he paced back and forth in front of his Rhodes Scholar Award, framed prominently at eye height. The Leader of the Opposition had a small office. Visitors were wise enough to leave enough room for Dougie *Do Right* to pace. "How come we are about 12 percent be-bloody-well-hind the government? When a week ago we were almost nine ahead. How come? Eh? Have you any idea? Eh? Tell me, come on, I need to bloody-well-know!"

"It's their PR team Dougie, I don't know how they did it. They not only stole most of our ideas but made theirs look original ... and ..."

"And what?"

"... and look really good." Ex-union boss and now upmarket lawyer, Wal *Hatchet* Stevens, adjusted his belt. He had overdone it at lunch time, had a touch of heartburn, should not have eaten two main courses, but still, in his position the rank-and-file paid for it.

Doug continued to pace. "Hell, Hatch, we had them on health, remember? I mean, in 12 years they have reduced our hospitals into a shambles, worse than a wharfie's piss-up. Only bankers, mining bosses and judges can afford to have basic health care, all at the expense of working Australians, our members! We had a plan, Hatch. Even the ham-fisted swinging voters could see that it was a real ripper, and then the government copy it and make us look like scammers."

The Leader of the Opposition had put absolutely everything into this campaign and they had looked so good. A week ago, the public was supporting them - with their scheme to rebuild public schools, tax-relief incentives for pensioners and the disabled, as well as a popular plan for real jobs for aboriginals, and above all, bringing Australia's young service people home from war zones. Most incredible of all they had a plan to keep the ABC free from the unstoppable advertisers. And now, the government had not only managed to ridicule all those incentives, but had stolen them almost to the letter, reworded them and released them as their own initiatives. The public had changed sides again, all in the space of a week.

"Bloody hell," sighed Dougie. Defeat hovered above him as he stepped to the window and looked out, hands clasped behind his back.

Hatch stood, "Don't worry comrade we'll think of something. I'll get the spinners to come in." He quickly smiled at his own joke.

Doug Do-Right, turned, shook his head slowly and frowned. The meeting was over.

Wal *Hatchet* Stevens strolled out; he tried to keep the smile from his outward demeanour. The job of the Leader of the Opposition looked like it had his name on it. Prime Minister one term away.

∞

On a golf course surrounded by perfect shades of green and blue, two immaculately dressed men stood leaning against a golf buggy.

Media mogul, Gary Ridge rubbed his right ear. "I think it's time to make the public aware of a few facts, mate, eh?"

Gary's irritation had increased markedly when he heard the decision the Miller-Anderson government had taken in opposing his recent indication to procure the last two remaining newspapers in Australia.

He continued, "Hell, Knobby, I don't want to have to give up my Aussie passport and become an American do I? Just to purchase what is rightfully mine, eh?"

David *Knobby* Clark smirked. He had been speaking to a certain Labour Party spinner who had assured him that Gary Ridge's desire to purchase any of the remaining TV and radio networks, would be looked upon sympathetically - for the odd piece of favourable publicity.

"Yep, the Libs are getting a bit big for their boots alright Gaz. Time for a change of government, what do you think?"

He walked over and placed the ball on the tee; with purpose and skill he thwatted the ball into the blue. Both men shielded their eyes and watched the white speck slowly bounce on to a smooth green.

Always the lobbyist playing both sides of the fence, David Clark turned around and looked at the newspaper man.

They acknowledged each other with the slightest of nods and broad smiles.

The end

Observe warnings

Experience should dictate

The enemy within

A BAD DAY

"What could possibly go wrong on a day like this?"

Braddo spoke to his faithful dog Kenneth who was at his most intelligent at that hour of the morning. This day was no exception; his nose was wet and his tail was on the go. Kenneth looked at his master and grimaced. Although only a dog, he had a way of knowing.

Braddo should have been able to tell that something was amiss too, but he was nursing a slight hangover and clearly was not at *his* best at that hour. If truth had it, he rarely was. His conscious thought of, *What could go wrong on a day like this?* must have given God the idea to organize the day in the opposite direction as a test.

The house was in its usual state of, at best, disorganisation, or at worst, a disgraceful mess. Braddo shook the cobwebs from his head and started clearing the sink to wash the previous night's dishes. He frowned at Kenneth. "I think I'd better go and renew my drivers' licence today."

Kenneth nodded and licked his chops.

Braddo cupped his hand around his mouth and whispered, "I'm off for a dad an' Dave," and he wandered off for a shower and a shave. He downed a few paracetamols as well. Kenneth knew things were not right. As far as he was concerned, Braddo did this sort of thing quite often, like having hangovers and sinks full of dishes, but this day had a strange feel about it.

After all the preening was completed, Braddo wandered around the place grabbing his wallet, keys and some other bits and pieces. He found the car keys in his jeans on the floor and then headed out to the car. Later, when he reflected on that day, it was about then that things went a little skew-whiff.

There was a mild hiccup first up when he turned the ignition key. The car would not start. As he went to lift the bonnet, he noticed that one of the front tyres was as flat as a pizza base.

"Stuff me gently," he grumbled, making a weak effort to clean the battery terminals.

Kenneth looked on.

The terminals were corroded and he had known about it for months and the battery had been on the way out for some time as well. Also, the tyres were worn and a flat was on the cards sooner or later. Braddo was not the sort of person to blame others when things went wrong, well not when it was his fault anyway. The wheel was changed amidst a colourful vocabulary of swear words and he managed to get the vehicle running by roll starting backwards down the driveway.

Kenneth continued to observe all this from the comfort of the front verandah, happy enough to not get involved in the problems of his *Dad*.

Braddo headed for town. There were few parks available but eventually he found one near the Registrar of Motor Vehicles. Only having notes in his wallet, he had to scratch around on the floor of the car for some time before he found the correct change for the parking meter. After a short stroll to the building, he made his way through the double glass doors and lined up at the **Drivers' Licence Renewals** counter.

Braddo chuckled contemptuously when he saw the sign, **Fast Lane – have your licence and relevant papers ready.** It was obvious that there was absolutely nothing resembling speed, or in fact movement, beyond a slow, depressing shuffle in the only lane for renewals.

In the world of people and personalities, Braddo was generally an easy-going sort of person and had recovered quickly from the earlier problems. Whilst standing in line he chatted with the young man in front of him, who was bitter about the delay. The bloke constantly referred to *them* and *they*, who were obviously the management of the Registrar of Motor Vehicles.

He turned around to Braddo and grizzled, "They should get more bloody staff on 'ere, this is piss weak, I'm not gunna put up with this any bloody longer." At that precise moment his turn came and he was facing the wrong way.

The lady behind the counter frowned because someone had the audacity to hold her up. "Next!"

This slowed the line up even more.

After standing for another five minutes because the punter did not have his paperwork ready, in addition to the original 25 minutes or so, Braddo's turn finally came.

"Next please!" was almost spat from the very official lady whose frown wiggled her wire rimmed prisms. Her hair was tied up into such a severe bun that her forehead looked almost shiny between frowns. The frown came and went as she examined the licence.

"I'm sorry sir, but your licence has expired and you have to go over to that line over there and they will fix you up."

He looked blankly at her, thinking perhaps that she had misread the situation.

"Why can't I just pay my money and renew it here?"

"I'm sorry sir but government regulations say that a new application has to be made and this line is for renewals only."

"But ... er ... surely this *is* a renewal, isn't it?"

"Yes, sir," she sighed acidly, "but your licence has expired."

The man behind him mumbled irritably, "Come on mate, we 'aven't got all day, some of us 'ave got jobs to go to, y'o, orright?"

So Braddo grasped his expired licence back with a roll of his eyes and moved to the line in question. After another 15 minutes waiting in a line with other unfortunates of the great unwashed, his turn came.

He was silly enough to whisper out of the corner of his mouth to a young woman who was trying unsuccessfully to control her three children, "You little beauty!" He clenched his fist in victory.

Braddo remembered this comment as being significant because when he related the story to a couple of mates at the pub sometime later, he was convinced that God must have picked up on it.

When he handed his licence to a young lady behind the counter she stated, "Mmm, I'm sorry sir but before we can renew this driver's licence, we have to have your birth certificate or a current drivers' licence."

"But they said over there that you would renew it here."

Her sigh had class distinction. "Of course, we *can* sir, but we need some form of ID."

He retorted, "But surely this licence shows that I am me." It seemed as clear as day, to him anyway as he pointed to the licence and then his face.

"That may be the case, sir, but the licence has expired and government regulations state that we cannot renew the licence on an expired licence without the correct documentation. You are lucky you came in now because you only have 48 hours to renew, otherwise you have to sit for your licence all over again."

"Again?"

"Yes, sir, you have 24 hours left."

Braddo replied with an edge, attempting to hide his growing irritation, "Well look, *You*, I have a Medibank card and a credit card. I'm sure they will do, along with my expired licence which has a photo of me, which is *obviously* me, that should do it. What do ya reckon?"

He looked at her firmly, but there was the slightest edge of pleading in his demeanour. She picked up on his fragility like a bitch sensing a threat around her pups.

"I'm sorry sir but we cannot renew your licence due to government regulations ... and I'm not *You*, alright? There are standards of address you know."

He felt like retaliating but was quick enough to realise that it would not help his case one bit. Also, he was aware that she was quite a good-looking sort and as he knew, good looking women could get away with almost anything with the average Australian bloke.

She added, "You have to provide your birth certificate. Next!"

Dismissed and dejected, Braddo ambled from that line and stood with the *forever blamed* to contemplate his situation. He lit up a cigarette because others in that area had started the trend in front of the plastic nicotine-stained **Thanks for not smoking** sign. Having a smoke made him feel slightly better, although it was hardly a protest. He had to renew his licence, so he knew he had to go home and try to find his birth certificate. Dodging kids, who were having the time of their lives, and the crowd of unfortunates, he headed out the double doors.

When he arrived at his car a parking inspector was leaning on the mudguard writing out a ticket.

"Hey, that's a bit rough, mate I'm only about a minute late."

The officer replied smoothly, "I'm sorry sir, but you are nearly 10 minutes overdue, may I suggest that you get your watch repaired."

The city official turned and walked off. Braddo glared after him and mumbled as many filthy words as he could get into the one breath. Even so, Braddo knew that it was his fault. The meter had expired and he only had himself to blame. Gloomy again, he jumped into the driver's seat and hit the starter.

CLICK!

"Root me dead!" he yelled in frustration banging the steering wheel with the heel of his hands, temporarily forgetting where he was. His window was down and an elderly lady, who was overseeing her red-faced Jack Russell trying to squeeze a hammerhead out of its bottom, glared at him as if it was his fault her dog was about to pass out. He shook his head, climbed out of the front seat, lifted the bonnet and fiddled about with the terminals. It was hopeless, the battery was dead.

Grumbling, he walked angrily to the Discount Batteries and Tyres place, some ten minutes away. After looking hopefully at several of the staff who pretended to be busy, and being forced to listen to very loud commercial radio, he was finally served. The new battery, fully charged, cost considerably more than he figured it should but there was no choice. The man in the grey dust coat charged him an extra $30 as a deposit on the return of the old battery which was deemed to be a trade in.

Braddo asked, "Hey mate, don't s'pose you could, er, give us a lift back to my car- it's only just up the road."

The bloke looked at him and tilted his head, "Hey Bud, whattya think we run 'ere, a taxi service? We don't have no time to be running no punters nowhere. Can't ya see we're flat out?"

Poor old Braddo could not do much about it as he had already paid for the battery, so he grabbed it off the counter and struggled back to his car. Naturally it was uphill most of the way and by the time he arrived, time had ticked by. Things did not look good. Leaning against the vehicle, grinning as he wrote out another ticket, was the parking inspector.

Braddo was deflated. "Hey mate, ya can't give me a ticket. I've already got one, don't ya remember?"

The officer looked at him and smiled. "Oh yes sir, I certainly *do* remember."

"But mate ... er sir, I can't get two tickets ... er can I? Besides my car is immobile and I couldn't move it even if I wanted to, which I do. Look, my car wouldn't start and I had to get another battery. See, right here."

"That's not my problem, sir, as far as I'm concerned, you've broken the law, full stop. There are council regulations you know; I mean we must have rules and regulations otherwise it'd be chaos around the place. Anyway, I can't pick and choose who I do and don't write tickets out for. I'm bound by rules and regulations."

He winked and strolled off, in the search of other lesser beings who did not know their rights. Braddo skinned his knuckles and mixed the blood with grime but finally got the car going. On the way he noticed Mr Parking Inspector and he stuck his head out the window and yelled, "I bet you wouldn't write out a ticket for a Mercedes driver ... ya mongrel."

Little did Braddo know that Mr Parking Inspector considered such occasions highlights in his working week.

It took a full half hour to get home because of roadworks and after considerable trouble and considerable conflict with himself as to whether he should have a joint or not, Braddo found his birth certificate. He grabbed all the documents that were scattered around in a drawer, including an old out of date passport, wrongly assuming that it would establish the real him. In better spirits he decided not to have a smoke because he had the feeling that he needed to be on the ball back at the Registrar. That was Braddo, he was capable of being sensible if the need was there.

Kenneth just lay around and licked his private parts, and observed his master. There was always hope that his *Dad* would remember to pick up some bones for him as the dry dog food was getting to be a bit boring. He was not game to kill another one of the neighbours' chooks after the belting he got last time. That was ages ago when he was barely older than a pup. Braddo had threatened to shoot him, so even if he was really hungry, he would not do that again. The last resort was Shovel Shanks, the old codger next door who gave him a bone or two every now and then. Kenneth wagged his tail and nuzzled Braddo a few times to shake his memory.

On the way back to town Braddo nearly had an accident as his eyes spent too much time zeroing in on a young woman in tights pushing a pram along the footpath. He was a sucker for the female form but it made him feel much happier. Demonstrating infinite patience, he eventually found a parking spot, making sure to stick money in the meter and further making sure to remember the time. It was beginning to be an expensive day for Braddo.

He walked quickly back to the Registrar and through the double doors. *His lane* was devoid of people and there was a handwritten little sign that said, **CLOSED - use other counter** which was the original *Fast Lane*. So, he lined up again in that lane realizing that he would have to be ready for the bureaucratic nightmare when his turn came.

His turn finally did come after what seemed like light years and as predicted the lady with the severe bun and glasses, barked rudely, "I'm sorry sir but you must go to that line over there, this lane is for renewals only." Then she looked at him more closely, looked at his expired licence and continued, "Didn't I see you earlier sir?"

He said nothing but felt he had to glare at her, even though he knew deep down that he was no match for the more experienced older woman.

Then he said, "Look lady, I may look a bit thick but that line is closed," as he gestured towards the empty line and what he considered to be a ridiculous sign.

She looked even more severe, if that was possible. "Be patient sir, we are in the process of streamlining this department, there's a restructure happening at the moment."

He mumbled under his breath, "There's a long way to go then, ya bloody stupid bitch."

She did not hear him but at least she got the message that this particular customer was not pleased, even though 99% of the people who went in there probably felt the same.

"Maybe you'd like to take a seat sir, until our staff member arrives back."

Braddo peered beyond her through the open door to the room behind where several staff members were sitting drinking coffee and laughing. He went and sat down next to the **Thanks for not smoking** sign and lit up a cigarette, along with all the others; bikies, drug addicts, alkies and lower socios, who, like him in truth, could not get it together to send the money off by post and have the licence renewed before the due date.

Braddo was not sure what to do. By law he was driving with an expired licence and knowing that his biorhythms were out of kilter he knew that if anyone was going to be picked up by the police it would be him. However, he did not get the chance to worry or make a decision because the princess of *His lane* casually came to the counter, removed the obnoxious sign and said, "Can I help anyone?"

He had an answer for that but a slovenly looking bikie nearby beat him to it and said, "Take ya gear off and give us a bit of table top dancing, babe."

She was not meant to hear it but she did and went red. Laughter echoed around the depressing government office and gave the place a huge lift, only for a moment though and only for the waiting unwashed. Three quarters of the people who were sitting and standing around killing time ran helter skelter to her counter. With the clash of desperate bodies Braddo came in third. The poor little fellow in front of him was Asian and he was even less of a match for the princess than Braddo. As his understanding of English was not good, he ended up being referred to the **Information** counter, where there was no one in attendance. The young man wandered over there, looking in all directions, totally bewildered.

Braddo did feel a bit sorry for the bloke and under different circumstances may have offered to help but he was not in the mood for political correctness as it was his turn next.

The princess took her time and scanned his paperwork. "Sir, this licence has expired and we need some verification to show us that this person is really you … can someone verify that this birth certificate belongs to you? It is an extract, not the original, and we require due to government regulations …"

Braddo was the sort of bloke who took quite a while to get worked up but he was now on the verge of exploding. He took a couple of deep breaths. "But I am me, I've got every sort of ID ever invented and I can assure you that this is bloody-well me."

She looked up and replied, "There's no need for abusive language, sir. Look, anyone can come in here and be anyone they want to be. Do you have any other ID with a photo of yourself because this licence has expired?"

"Would my baby book do?" he retorted sarcastically and proceeded to hold up his baby book for the others to see for a laugh, even though he was not in a happy mood.

She gave him a complex glance and said, "There's no need for this, sir."

Just then he remembered his passport and gave it to her.

"I'm sorry sir this passport has expired."

"Look lady, I know it has expired but see that little picture, that's me, see. Also, here's my Medibank card, see, my signature, see, this credit card, see, the signature, that's me. The birth certificate is me, see, it's signed by a JP – in this office. Go on, ask me where I was born, come on, ask me the year, get me to sign something and compare the signatures. Look, this is insane, how else can I prove that I am me … this is bloody outright ridiculous."

Braddo had blurred past the point of being able to be reasonable. He surprised himself somewhat by saying loudly and firmly, "I *demand* to see your supervising officer, *right now!*"

The wife bashers, drug addicts, lower socios and children in the space clicked to hush, hoping for a raucous confrontation.

Off balance, she stuttered, "Er ... excuse me, sir." She turned quickly, and briskly walked through the door.

The noise in the room returned to normal. After about five minutes, with the body odour and weight of the battlers lined up shuffling and sighing behind him, she returned, "This is rather unusual but I think on this occasion we can stretch the regulations."

With that she scribbled some information onto another form, asked him to fill it out and go over to the area marked, **PHOTO AREA - KEEP CLEAR**. He frowned at her feeling marginal relief that this whole pantomime was almost over. "Apology accepted," he breathed at her. He pushed the smile in her direction, thinking that under different circumstances, maybe down the pub, he would give her a try.

Focussing in on the warning sign about radiation gave him a shudder, but he hoped it was not high level so he filled out the form anyway and gave it to a bored young man with moons all over his face.

The pimply adolescent said in a dreamy, not-there voice, "Sit down on the stool, buddy, look at the camera and do not smile. Right?"

Braddo had no problem obliging him on the latter score as there was very little to raise a giggle about in this office, so he did the former as requested. The young man took the photo, demanded what seemed a huge amount of money for it and then told him to go and wait at the cashier's section. Evidently when his name was called out, he was expected to pay even more money.

So, back he went to the lower socios again. Braddo had to smoke to mask the fact that the body odour and other smells had gone up a notch, so he moved away and attempted a bit of a chat session with a nice-looking young woman. Unfortunately, it became clear she was not worth pursuing because her two kids were running all over the office annoying everyone. After 20 minutes and a few fags, his name was called out.

The sourest female he had ever seen in his life demanded money which was duly paid. There was no argument from him, he was just keen to get out of there. She handed him his licence; no smile came with it. Overjoyed was at the bottom end of how he felt but relief was close to first.

It had only taken most of the day. There was strong camaraderie among the punters and he waved to them, almost as mates, as they puffed away whilst entertained by watching the kids run wild. Braddo felt like a man might feel walking out of jail as he pushed his way through the double glass doors into the fresh air.

Fortunately, the parking inspector was nowhere near his vehicle as Braddo noticed that he was once again overdue. It occurred to him that maybe his luck was going to change but he dismissed the thought quickly in case God was tuned in.

Down the road he noticed the Inspector writing out a ticket for the young mother whom he had met at the Registrar of Motor Vehicles. As he drove off, he tooted, stuck his finger up his nose with his head out the window and yelled, "You should run for parliament, mate."

On the way home he remembered with a jolt that he had to take back the battery to retrieve his deposit, so he had to do a U turn. He pulled up out the front of Discount Batteries and Tyres and struggled in with the old dirty battery. The man behind the counter was different from the earlier attendant. The new man, wearing an American baseball cap with *Bulldozer* written on it, did his best to look busy until it was clear that no one else was going to serve Braddo, but he still hung on. The commercial radio station volume still hammered out adverts with the occasional popular number.

Braddo had had enough of everything. "Hey mate?"

"You right there, buddy? What can we do for ya, bud?" the bloke said through a sea of roadmap eyes and extreme disinterest.

Braddo replied, "I've come to get my deposit back for the battery I bought earlier."

"Right Bud, got ya receipt? No receipt? Sorry, bud, can't give no money back to no one without no receipt."

"Oh, yeah, shit, I've got the receipt here somewhere. Hang on." Braddo rifled his pockets and concluded quickly that it must be in the car somewhere. "Be back in a mo, must be in the car."

He went out and searched the car from top to bottom to no avail. Extremely frustrated and angry with the world he went back in and tried to reason with the attendant but the man would not budge. Just then the original bloke came in looking busy.

Braddo exclaimed with relief, "Hey mate remember me? I brought me old battery back but I can't find the receipt."

He took his time to look up. "Mmm … yeah, I remember you; you're the bloke that thinks we are a taxi service. Listen, we can't do nothing without the proper paperwork. There are regulations here ya know. We just can't go givin' out money to anyone who walks in here, now can we."

Even though Braddo was only five feet ten and weedy at that, he was about to throw the battery over the counter at the two officious retail staffers, when who should walk in but his old mate Skiddy *Skidmarks* Skidmore. At first Skiddy did not see Braddo as he had his attention focused behind the counter.

"Howz it goin' *Dozer*?" yelled Skiddy. Then he saw Braddo. "Aaaaah! Braddo, how the hell are ya mate?"

Braddo's eyebrows scrunched up and he mumbled with a degree of venom, "I'd be a fuck of a lot better if these pricks gave me my money back for the deposit on this battery."

Jim *Dozer* Kruger interjected, "Hey, you blokes know each other? Ah well, that's all right. Tell ya what I'll do then, we can stretch the rules then, here's ya money," and he elbowed the till. "Here ya go buddy, but we get all sorts here." No sorry.

Braddo snatched the $30 from the man behind the counter and pushed towards the door, "Buy you a beer, Skiddy, definitely one I owe ya." He held up his thumb and walked out.

The big fellow Skiddy looked a bit bewildered but mumbled to the swinging door, "Yeah, rightoh, mate. Yeah, no worries."

Braddo thought he would drop into the pub for a quiet beer, after all, as far as he was concerned, the shadows of the westerly sun were stretched far enough. Also, he'd had a very stressful, gruelling day. Stressful, stretched, and gruelling.

Braddo was only human.

Bewkers Buchanan was there holding up the bar and it was hard to avoid him. His eyebrows went up. "Ow ya doin' buddy?"

Braddo cringed but a reply was necessary, "Good, buddy, real good, real good buddy, you bet, swell and what's goin' down?"

Bewkers looked at Braddo as if there was something wrong with him. Braddo looked at him wondering if anyone spoke Australian around the place anymore.

"I'm on a mission, mate," he saluted and paced down to the end of the bar. He glanced back, Bewkers was so unconscious to the real world that he had snared another passer-by, so Braddo ordered a beer from *Dezi the Demon*, who it was rumoured was the greatest barman south of the Equator.

"How's ya life Braddo, looks like ya need a beer."

"That is the most truest thing I've heard today, mate."

Dezi nodded and went to serve others. Braddo found a spot on the verandah with Ben *Doggie* Bone and Eric *Bag* Barton and they talked about old times. They had a few laughs and a round each, which made Braddo think that things could easily be on the up.

Then he noticed Andrew Capper, known as *Andy Cap*, over in the corner with a group of rowdy fringe dole recipients. He appeared to be quite drunk and had not noticed Braddo, because if he had he would have snuck out. The Cap owed money to almost everyone, especially Braddo who covered the ground quickly and was on the Cap in a flash.

"G'day Cap, howz it goin'? Remember me, Cap … eh?"

"Aah … yeah, g'day …"

Braddo tried to look tough. "I don't suppose you could see your way clear to fix us up with the money you owe Tint and me from the job at the Point?"

"Oh … yeah, er no, sorry mate but I'm broke at the moment. I haven't forgotten."

"Yeah, you're always broke when it comes to payin' me but ya always seem to have enough money for fags and booze." Braddo had downed a few and he'd had the day he'd had.

Out of the blue, one of the Cap's fringe dole bludger mates, at least one axe handle across the shoulders, and short on atoms between the ear drums, pushed to the front.

"Who're you, you're not botherin' me old mate Cap, are ya?"

It all happened quickly; he pushed Braddo who spilt most of his beer and in the process managed to bump someone else leaning against the wall. Unfortunately, *the someone else* was, in the words Braddo used to his mates ages later on the verandah, the size of a house with a range of tattoos and a traditional blue singlet. He glared at Braddo who quickly apologised and pointed toward where the Cap's mob used to be. An apology was made again and Braddo quickly headed down the other side of the bar. He had one more drink on his own and then decided to go home.

It had been an eventful day and most of those events were stressful.

He only had what he would call a few, and he really did not think he was over the limit, or if he was, only just over, he would give it go. To be on the safe side he decided to go home the back way. Cops had never been seen out that way for ages, so chances were in his favour. He drove carefully, as any sensible drunk person would do and just as he thought he had made it to the relative safety of the outer back roads, there they were.

The Cops.

Braddo felt hot and cold in his spine. A female cop waved him down and asked in one of what Braddo had become familiar with several times that day, a polite, yet firm, official type of voice.

"Excuse me, sir, but have you been drinking?"

"Who me sir, er officer … er no, I don't drink."

Her glance in the dark did not waver. "Could you please show me your licence, sir?"

"Yes of course, I've got a brand new one right here," smiled Braddo proudly, beginning to think that producing a brand-new licence would solve everything. It did not take long to realize that he had lost his wallet, or misplaced it, along with his licence, somewhere along the journey.

Braddo just sat there for a moment wondering what to say.

She stood back, not releasing her gaze for a second, "Would you please step out of the car, sir."

Mr Police Officer was standing a couple of yards back. He folded his arms.

Braddo replied bravely but weakly, "Look, it was here a while ago."

Ms Police Officer repeated, "I won't ask you again, sir, will you please step out of the vehicle."

Mr Police Officer who was wearing riding boots, with no sign of a horse around, and a Gestapo type hat, strolled over with the breathalyser. "Would you please blow into this tube, sir."

Braddo knew he was in strife. He was a little bit pissed and thought the better of a wise crack. He made a feeble effort to blow in the bag.

The female officer said, "If you continue in this malingering fashion, sir, we may consider taking you down to the station and you can do it properly there."

Having no choice, he blew properly. Perhaps his luck had changed or the machine was faulty because the reading was .09.

Mr Policeman Officer said sternly, "You're over the limit, sir, and I may have to take you to the station for further tests."

"But sir, it's only .01 of a percent, that's nothing," offered Braddo, who had experienced a high and a low, all within a couple of seconds. Both the officers walked away out of earshot and there was babble on the radio he could not decipher. He was left standing for a moment or two.

They came back. She said, "Could you please give me your name and address."

He did, easily.

Her smile was measured. "Now sir, in addition to the drink-driving there's also the matter of your licence."

"Officer," pleaded Braddo, "I just had it renewed today, I can prove it, or …"

"Sir, it must be your lucky day. We just verified that this vehicle is registered to you and your licence was renewed today. We have decided to not bother taking you to the station because by the time we do, your blood alcohol level would probably drop to below the legal limit of .08%."

Braddo had to stop himself from saying, "Listen here gorgeous lips, I can do without days as bloody lucky as this." He nodded and began to climb back into the car.

Mr Police Officer put his hand very firmly on Braddo's shoulder.

"I'm sorry sir, but as you are over the limit, we cannot allow you to be in control of a motor vehicle."

Braddo pleaded, "But officer I live several miles from here, how am I going to get home?"

"Walk of course," the officer replied with the slightest of smirks.

"But sirs, I'm only a little over and by the time I get behind the wheel I'll be below the level, have a heart, it's a long walk."

Ms. Police Officer took a step closer and looked straight into his eyes. Even though it was dark, Braddo thought that she had lovely eyes. He got a faint whiff of perfume.

"Maybe sir would like to perform another test, down at the station."

"Er ... no sir ... um Officer. No thanks, I'll be off." With that he locked the car.

"There is the matter of the licence," she continued, "you still have to produce your licence at the nearest police station." She paused for effect and then added with obvious pleasure, "Within 24 hours."

Braddo pretended to smile, turned, and trudged off, stumbling in the dark.

By the time he arrived home he was tired and worn out. Kenneth growled at him because his sleep had been disturbed. And his dinner was late or more than likely non-existent. Braddo had had enough, after all, he reasoned, if you could not take it out on your dog, what was there left in life?

"Look, you fucking useless prick of a dog, I've had a mongrel of a day and if you don't show me some respect, I'll kick the living shit outta ya!"

Whether it was the word *mongrel* or just the straight-out anger, Kenneth realized that he was in the poo and he cowered off to a corner with his tail between his legs.

Braddo rang and just caught Dezi the Demon tidying up at the pub but was told that no one had handed in a wallet. He mentioned that people usually do, but there is never any money in them. Dezi threw in, *Ha ha* at the end.

"Thanks a fucking lot, Dezi. If it turns up, please let me know, alright?"

"Yeah, not a prob, mate, see ya."

∞

He had an uncomfortable night, made better or worse, depending on how you looked at it, by demolishing a few stubbies, and half a bottle of sherry that he kept in the house for emergencies such as this. Also, he'd had a few smokes as well.

Poor old Braddo was not sure how to even start to face having to go through obtaining a new licence again, let alone replacing credit cards. Of course, his meagre amount of money was gone as well. He finally knew what deep depression was and could almost picture himself taking his own life. Deciding suicide would be an over-reaction he rationally concluded that this had been a very bad day.

Stumbling into bed late, Braddo woke the next morning with a frightful headache. He did not exactly wake but was woken by the shrilling of the phone.

It was Dezi, who yelled into the phone, as his whole life consisted of yelling at people, "The cleaner has just handed in your wallet and, guess what mate, I'll go ya halves, it's got money, credit cards, frenchies, and a brand-new licence. Hey, why don't ya smile when ya get ya photo taken, ya miserable prick. I'll stick it in the safe. Just pop in anytime."

It hurt Braddo to talk but he mumbled gratefully, "Thanks mate, I'll be in later when I pick up me car."

Just then little Kenneth eased his way, low to the ground, into the kitchen, looking very apologetic. He smiled with his eyes in anticipation. Braddo had a severely sore head but he had a feeling that today was going to be a better day and not wanting to challenge God he kept the thought to himself.

The end

Real time escalates

Trust survival skills

Tomorrow may be better

PULSE

Alternate streetlights flickered. No taxis, not that Stephanie was game to get in one at such an early hour. Her panic had subsided in the last couple of minutes; however, there was still some distance to her home. She recalled last night being volunteered for the nightshift, which meant a double shift, starting at the time her day should have ended. That was hours ago.

The poor bus driver. Three hoods dragged him out of the bus and were kicking him in the head. They had not seen her hiding behind a seat, and as she waited for the opportunity to escape one of them shoved a samurai sword straight through the driver's neck. They were far too busy kicking and jumping on the poor man, so she seized her chance to escape.

Fortunately, Stephanie wore sensible shoes and was quick on her feet; fear gave her the extra edge. As she ran from the bus, one of the three chased her for about 20 metres, but he was a blob, drunk and bombed. Sweaty heat and the crystal cold in her spine pushed her to run faster than ever in her life. Lungs screamed and heart thumped and her mouth felt like clag. Just as she entered a section of streetlights that did not work, a vehicle turned into the street, accelerated past her, and stopped with a screech. The V8 rust bucket ute burbled; exhaust wafting burnt oil smoke. The driver dropped the clutch into reverse, smoke billowed, rubber burnt and the car screeched and snaked backwards. Stephanie leapt with fright.

A youth with a Mohawk haircut, hanging out the window bellowed, "Hey honey, what's a fuckin' sheila like you doing out here alone? You must be beggin' for it!"

The other two whooped with laughter. Stephanie blindly did a right angle turn through the overgrown plastic and cigarette-butt garden of a block of flats. In that click of time, the weak translucent caged globe above the front door gave her comfort. There was no time to think what would happen if the wire glass-reinforced doors were locked, but she managed to scamper into the dark foyer. The shrieking and the guffawing tracked her like a laser as she whipped around the corner. Then she saw it.

Self-control deserted her and a scream exploded from deep down. Someone had screwed a Chihuahua to the wall; a haggis stomach drooped out of a gash in front. Blood and innards stuck to the grubby wall and blobs of muck decorated the floor.

She stood in a trance, hands squeezing her ears, trying to claw in the screaming. The overhead light faltered a couple of times, then darkness. She may have wet herself, did not know, did not care and it did not matter anyway, her clothes were saturated with cold, tense sweat. Realisation dawned that she was in the land of the living once more when the light hiccupped, blinked, and came on again, pretending that it had never been off.

The louts out the front were yelling and throwing bottles and it was clear that she could not go that way. Stephanie looked hysterically in every direction with bulbous eyes, knowing there was a need to get going. *But where?*

That is when she heard it. A dull scraping noise, someone was dragging something behind them. The boiling, tingling hell of horror screwed to the wall in front, drew her stare, captivated her being. Pulses hammered every part of her body. Her feet froze to the floor. The shadow on the far wall materialised from around the corner.

"Aaaah, sorry love. Did I frighten you?"

Stephanie was stiff, just able to shake at the same time and unable to respond.

"I sometimes do frighten people, I mean, with this face." He pointed with a badly deformed hand to his grotesquely damaged face.

"Fire. Got caught in a fire. Only got one eye and one ear, my leg tends to drag a bit too, no nerves or feeling, and my fingers nearly burnt off on this hand ... oh, sorry love, my name is Albert, I'm the cleaner and caretaker here. Can't do a real job 'cos people get frightened by my appearance, have to work at night."

A tap dripped in the distance, long slow clicks. She stood petrified, unable to talk, unable to look at him, just past him. Seconds ticked by, the tap out the back continued to drip in slow motion.

"Oh, dear lord," he mumbled through a puffy mouth. "Look what someone has done to little Chico. I told Mrs Richards if she didn't stop her dog from piddling and pooping everywhere that someone would do something about it."

Stephanie blurted, "... Go ... got to ... gggo!"

Nervous energy spun her around, down the corridor and out the front door. The louts saw her and cheered, throwing a bottle that smashed on the wall near her head which forced a change in direction towards the back. She leapt a low hedge, nearly tripping, and rounded the corner. Fear spurred her on as she frantically looked for a place to hide. Fortunately, there was an alcove where the bins were gathered so she threw herself in there, hugging the shadows. It was the only choice as the louts rounded the corner.

"Where the fuck is the little harlot?" spat Mohawk.

"Aaaah, who gives a root, she was just a skinny little bitch anyway. I need a piss!"

The other animal staggered over near her, unzipped himself and started urinating almost on her foot. Stephanie's heart pummelled and her breathing sounded to her like an aqualung deep in the ocean. He had to hear it.

He burped loudly, fumbled with the zip, and then sluggishly turned around.

"Let's go dick-brain; she's well and truly fucked off now. I need a drink to replace the fluid I lost!"

They laughed and sleeked away.

Stephanie steeled herself to quell the shaking and her breathing slowly returned to somewhere near normal. Her mouth felt like dry flour. At least she was now together enough to try to think. Then, a scraping noise filtered from the area over near the wall. That frantic freezing fear returned. The silhouette of a cat leaped out from behind the bins on to the fence and over. Her heart bounced.

After a few moments, as a level of calm returned, she stepped out of the shadows. Anvil hands grabbed her and threw her against the wall. There was a dragging sound, his breath was putrid and grunting squeaking sounds came from the deep. He grabbed her again, this time by the hair and smashed her face into the wall. She could feel damage to her nose and loose pieces of teeth filled her mouth, blood burst everywhere.

Stephanie struggled for life with the strength of someone aware of the alternative. From the weak light of a window several houses away, the outline of Albert's horrible face, with his dead dog body odour loomed inches in front of her. He pawed her breasts and wrenched at her panties, grunting, and whining as frantically as she was fighting back. She clawed at his face as he pushed her backwards onto a ledge, smacking her head against the concrete wall. Her hand went out trying to break the fall, searching for something, anything, to hold on to. Nothing.

His right hand went to unzip his pants. Just then, her hand automatically closed around what felt like a tent peg or a piece of reinforcing rod. She plunged the rod with all her might into one of his eyes, not knowing or caring which was the good one. He bellowed like a wild animal, his body tensed like a spring for a few seconds, and then went limp. She could feel his warm blood dripping on her. There was a scream deep down inside but it could not come out even if she had wanted it to because of the weight of his body. She managed to roll him off and he thudded onto the ground like a damp bag of fertiliser. Stephanie tried to stand, boiling with fright and humiliation.

A light went on up on the third floor of the building next door. "Shuddup you bastards or I'll come down and cave ya fuckin' heads in with a piece of water pipe. Inconsiderate pricks!" The voice was brutal, heavy with liquor and very out of it. The window slammed shut and the light went off, leaving her to her own nightmare.

Her dress was ripped, panties torn to pieces and she had been lying in excrement, rotting food or a putrid, decomposing animal.

One eye was full of blood or closed, her nose was surely broken and she spat out pieces of teeth.

Albert had not moved. Her wits returned a little, she crept to the safety of the shadows again, hyperventilating, breathing in thrusts.

"Come on Steph," she croaked in a voice that was not familiar. "You can do this, you can do it, you can do it, you've taken control ..."

Her heart thundered against her ribs and blood pulsed at the ends of every artery. Stephanie willed herself to think about what a bastard of a day it had been. Not only drawing the night shift, but thinking that when she left work at midnight, the hardship would be over. *Bloody hell, how could I even* ... For her, midnight was the beginning of a hell that no one could ever imagine. She hoped that when the sun finally came up this terror would end.

Forced breathing slowly coordinated with her beating heart. Screeching tyres out the front indicated the louts were going elsewhere, but she was not prepared to take the risk of going that way. It was madness to stay where she was any longer. She opened the gate, figuring that it must go in the direction of the back street. She started shaking again. *Come on Steff, it's okay, come on ...*

She felt a survival instinct to move. The click of the gate latch behind was crisp. A dog barked, deep and nasty, coming her way. She jumped and tripped at the same time landing almost head first in a drain. It felt like a crocodile grabbing her shoulder and she was aware of the sound of cracking bone. Frantic and with every ounce of strength she hit the animal on the head with a brick. The Rottweiler bellowed, made a side-to-side flapping sound with a collar jingle, and came at her again, enraged from the bash on the head. That snip of a second allowed her to crawl backwards into the concrete pipe, but the dog bit her on the face as she tried to fend it off with a piece of wood. At the same time, she managed to jam a large oil drum in the entrance. The enraged animal continued to gnash and paw at the steel drum. Warm blood began to soak her torso and her shoulder hurt like nothing she had ever experienced. The pain kept her alive and alert. Instant vomit burbled from down low and burst out of her mouth like a geyser. The guard dog barked, gnashed its teeth, and snarled menacingly, using the intimidation of its position, excited by the instant reek of stomach contents everywhere. Above all the filth, she could smell and feel the incredible power of the animal. The view through a small gap, with the aid of a small moon behind, revealed its block-like head, snarling and attacking the steel edge of the drum. Evil eyes glinted with the occasional flash of nasty teeth dripping goop below quivering jowls and cheeks.

Stephanie kept up the mantra; she was going to be alright and safe for the moment. The relief in that small safety den was so overwhelming that she started sobbing. The hope of a new day gave her strength of will, if only for the immediate time.

The dog continued to growl like distant thunder, paw the drum and occasionally bark, but as her sobbing quietened it appeared to lose interest and wandered away.

Reality returned and she realised she was an animal, trapped like an animal. The dog stirred every now and again, letting her know that he was still there. She knew it was a male dog. The shaking started again, even though it was not a cold night; and the pain in her shoulder slowly turned to numbness. Sometime later, minutes or hours, there was a noise at the gate.

Stephanie was about to yell, "Here, over here, please help me!" but the sound of the voice stopped her dead.

"Hey, Hitler!" The voice growled like the dog, and was heavy with drink. "Come on, you lazy bastard of a dog, time to go on patrol. Them blue tongue lizards still in the drain, eh?"

There was the sound of a chain rattling. "Oi! Get over here, you stinkin' bastard of a dog! Oi, here or I'll bash ya!"

A minute later, they were gone.

She must have passed out again, because when consciousness surfaced, greasy, pea soup light trickled into the pipe entrance. Stephanie felt complete hopelessness; she was weak and sore and the shaking tremored inside. A numbness and weariness of body threatened to immobilise her. She knew the next few minutes were crucial to survival. She calculated that the dog and the man were gone and the gate was open. She had to chance it. With enormous effort, she rolled the drum out of the way and dragged herself out. Standing up took every atom of her strength.

Stephanie then became aware of her appearance. Covered in congealed blood and filth, her dress and top were ripped almost beyond modesty, she had no underwear and she noticed with alarm that there were no shoes on her bleeding, lacerated feet. Vision was just possible out of one eye; her nose was broken and it seemed as if half her teeth were missing or cracked. Her face was a battered, swollen, torn mess. Sharp stabs of pain were a reminder that her shoulder was crushed and misshapen, and several pieces of flesh hung down like bacon rind.

There were no tears left.

She gingerly made her way to the back gate and stepped through. A shadow crossed her path. Fear pricked her soul; for a nano-second, she thought she was in hell. She was too tired and weak to react.

It was only the shadow of young girl on a bike riding past singing.

She stood there wretched, just outside the gate. About 20 metres along the road two officers were leaning up against a police car talking to an old lady with a Golden Retriever puppy, straining on the end of a lead and wagging his tail.

Stephanie felt the sun on her.

It was a new day.

The end

Willpower is needed

Sometimes -

No record of overdose

HASHISH FUDGE

"Here, have a toke," grunted Baz, smoke billowing out his nostrils. He held out a joint at arm's length.

"I'd love to man, but I got emphysem-i-a, can't smoke no more." Gaz wheezed the last few words for effect.

"Come on man, don't be as weak as. That's un-Australian rejecting a tug on a spliff. I've got some top-quality hash here." Black burn holes decorated the front of his *Take a Trip* tee shirt.

"Nah, can't, wish I could man, but I'll get lung cancer if I ever smoke again," replied Gaz. "That's what Dr Harris said anyway." He re-tied his Hendrix style psychedelic headband and re-arranged black Afro springs.

"What would Dr Haz know anyway?" teased Baz. "Got to die of something man, come on."

"Nup. Hey man, I got a serious willpower thing going down here, man. Have some sympathy, man."

Baz took another drag and held the smoke in, which caused him throaty struggles that ended with rich bellowing coughing. When he had recovered, he had a go at speaking. "Why don't you make some hash cookies, or cake or something, because I tell you, man, it's real good stuff, get my drift?"

Gaz's eyes brightened but it was hard to notice through his Dame Edna sunglasses. "Hey, that's a great idea man, how do you, like make, whatever you make?"

Baz looked at his mate through roadmap eyes. He scratched his bald head and fingered the woven leather thong above dried apricot ears that he told people held his hair in place. "I've got a recipe book here somewhere written by Cheech and Chong on how to make cakes, cookies, fudge, you name it."

His speech was as slow as a drunken snail. Normally, Gaz would not have noticed, because he would have been ripped to the eyeballs, too, but now he was as alert as a kelpie at dawn because of his serious medical condition.

"Right, where's that book?" Gaz had made up his mind. He unfolded his stalk like frame from the armchair.

Baz could only point to the bookcase, he was so stoned, speech was a struggle. "Er, over there."

Gaz pushed the sunglasses up over the headband into his hair and gave an impression of a serious silly walk over to the bookcase. He ran his hand along the spines.

"What have we got now, mmm? Flowers? No, man, who gives a root about them, don't want that. How to make mango chutney? Naah, who cares?" Piano player's fingers spidered the spines. "Ah! Here we are. The complete book of cooking THC by Cheech and Chong. Hell, man, looks like there's cartoons too, as well as recipes. Get a load of dem guys, got a picture on the cover from that movie, *Up in Smoke*, wow!"

Baz tried to speak. "I remember when we made these dope cookies ..."

Gaz tried to be polite. "Uh, yeah?"

"Hell yeah, anyway, we used about 2 ounces of Noosa heads ..." He drifted off, eyes chasing the inside of his head.

Gaz, meantime, was flicking through the book. "Here we are. Hashish Fudge. Listen to this Baz, Cheech says, you need good quality hash to start with -- what's the stuff you got like? Er, Baz?"

"Aaaaaah, boy-oh-boy a Lincoln Toy, did we get ripped, we went ...

"Baz, we've moved on from there. I asked you what the hash was like."

"Uh? Oh ... yeah, so unbelievably good I can't believe it, super unrealistic, almost trippy, man."

Gaz unfolded himself again. "Well, man, I'd better go and get some, now, shouldn't I?"

Baz could only nod as he took another drag and coughed richly.

Gaz thought that his old mate Baz could easily give up smoking too. With the cough he had it was a wonder he was not used to scare fruit bats away from mango trees.

∞

Several hours later, Gaz arrived back at the house after visiting Laz, who was *THE MAN* who kept everyone on Freak-me-out-Street supplied with artificial stimulants. As could be expected, Baz had just finished another hash joint.

"Hey man … just having a look at …"

Gaz noticed Baz was reading, or more correctly staring at a Furry Freak Brothers comic. He knew Baz could sit for hours with a comic open to the same page.

"What's that intellectual stuff you're reading, man, mmm? No, don't bother man, I'm astute enough to see you're on a mission inside your head. Get out of my way, man, not that you need to, judging by how ineffective you would be if you made the slightest attempt at negating me, man."

That rapid fire of intellectual dialogue was too much for Baz. The easiest option for him was not to react. He did not and could not.

Gaz untangled himself and assaulted a chair. He opened the book at the table and read aloud.

"Mmmm, now, it says, *heat up at least 20 grams of good quality hash by poking a pin into a chunk of it and heating over a candle. Wave the product across the flame to toast it. Make sure not to burn it -- at the sight of the slightest smoke, remove from flame. Allow to cool for a moment and then crumble into small pieces, preferably powder like.*"

"Hey man," interrupted Baz, rolling his bald head in Gaz's direction. He had the comic open to the same page and would probably not be capable of moving to the next page for the rest of the night. Waiting for him to make his point was like waiting to be served at a hardware shop at ten to five. "Don't burn it, man, just toast it, man, right?"

"Yeah, man, I am on top of it, orright, I got it. Now stand back, here goes."

He executed the first part of the operation smoothly, but Baz was intent on still being part of the process, even though he was not all there. "Now man, it says here in the ..."

"Hey, buzz off Baz; aren't you stoned enough, man?"

Baz tried to stand up, but fell back into the armchair. He tried to focus under eyelids that looked like half-drawn blinds. "Hey man, you can't never get too stoned, man."

Meanwhile, Gaz had crumbled the hash up, making sure to heed the tip to scrape every bit off his fingers in the process. He put sugar, milk, and cocoa into a saucepan. "Hey Baz, before I start, have we got a thermometer?"

It took Baz a few seconds to respond as his brain played ping-pong with his eyeball coordination. "Er, nup, not that I ... er ... hang on, yeah man, we got a rectal thermometer in the bathroom closet in the second aid kit."

"Rectal thermometer? Nah, man, don't worry about that, never know where that's been! I'll estimate 116°C. It says all but boil, she'll be as apples as. Here goes!"

He heated the mix, stirring until it started to boil. "Hey man," burped Baz in snail speak. "It says here to, like not boil ..."

"Yeah, I know that man, orright? Stir until boiling point, let sit and then whisk up again as it cools. I bloody-well know that, man. Keep your bald head out of the process man, I know what I'm doing, it's pretty hectic here in the kitchen. Get my meaning, like the temp is up in the decision-making process, okay?"

He removed the saucepan from the stove, waited a moment, added butter and a teaspoon of vanilla. His tongue stuck out the corner of his mouth like Winston Churchill's cigar, and his eyebrows declared acute concentration as he stirred vigorously; the mix went into a buttered tin.

"Hey Baz, gissa butcher's hook at that recipe again, man?" He covered the stove to the table in long purposeful strides like John Cleese and grabbed the book. "Mmm, yeah righto." He stroked his chin; eyebrows formed a straight line. Then he strode back to the sink, grabbed a knife, and set about marking the mixture in the tray to the portion sizes recommended by the book.

"Hey, man … hey man?"

"You said that, man."

"Yeah man, I wanna get one of them Cheech and Chong T-shirts, you know, the ones with …"

"Listen man, I haven't got time to listen to your gargle, man, I'm busy doing important work here, man." He rocked backwards and forwards on his heels admiring his handy-work like a professor who had just discovered life on Pluto.

"Not a bad job, even though I do say so myself, Baz. Had to get the sizes right, because Cheech says at the start of the recipe how important it is because of the chance of overdose by an inexperienced person out there in punter-land."

Baz tried to stand. "Hey, like wow man, let's get into it now."

"Wooo-aah! You're pretty ripped already man, and besides, the stuff has to cool down anyway."

He picked up the book, could not help laughing at the cartoon and flicked the page. At the top he noted, *Hashish Fudge comes with a severe warning.* There were two cartoons. One with Cheech eating a piece of fudge with a tick underneath.

The other cartoon showed Chong eating a piece of fudge and smoking a large joint. This cartoon had a red line through it. There was a caption underneath.

"Hey man, listen to this," offered Gaz, waving his index finger like a pushy holy man. *"Warning! Due to the heating of the hash and the addition of sugar, together with the boiling process, the THC level increases. It is therefore recommended that smoking dope of any kind before eating this fudge could result in an overdose.* See here too, man, Cheech says that nobody dies, if you follow the instructions. Chong says, *But hey man, I've never known of anyone dying, but it's got to be worth a try."*

Gaz unfolded his legs, did a praying mantis creep, and tangled over to his bald-headed mate. "Did you hear that, man, what Cheech says? I mean to say, we don't want to be knee deep in fly blown carcasses or stiffs around here, right man?"

Baz tried to stand up and fell back into the armchair. "Why, I don't give a root, man, I'm going with what Chong says. See? I'm not smoking at the moment, see, no joint here, right man? Hey? See? Come on, man."

Baz threw his hands in the air. One day into giving up was heavy on his mind, there were stress points everywhere. The decision was easy.

They both had a piece of the hashish fudge.

The end

Complacency

Has no place -

Against the clock

COUNTDOWN

The rickshaw lurched to a halt at the front entrance of the railway station.

The young driver produced a red betel nut smile. "Ticket, ticket, Malabar Express," and nodded in the direction of the grand stone archway. He launched a squirt of beetle juice into the corner of the step.

Melissa climbed out; sweat already glistened on her forehead. Relieved to still be alive after what felt like a sideshow dodgem car race from the hotel, she pulled out her money to pay. Other rickshaw drivers gathered around. They pretended not to stare at her now almost wet tee-shirt. Mel was glad of the bra but she knew she should not have worn shorts. A group of men sat cross-legged under the only tree, smoking bidis. Bollywood music whined from a drinks stall. On the other side of the steps, along the wall, a man in white skull cap and dhoti urinated into a pile of rubbish. A pi-dog watched without interest.

Melissa handed the driver the agreed rupees. "Thank you." She smiled her best.

"No problem, no problem," he said as he dragged out her rucksack.

A group of touts appeared, attracted to a walking wallet with an added bonus, a young western female on her own. They all talked at once offering advice and assistance. Some tried to touch her. She understood their innocence; young males just sniffing around. *Back off, will you?*

49

"No thank you, no thank you, I'm okay," she said firmly, hoisting the rucksack onto her shoulder. Her dark hair was tied back; sweat trickled down behind her ears.

The young hopefuls continued to nudge and talk.

"Thank you, I'm okay," she said, louder. *Not strong enough. Be more assertive, Mel.*

They paid no attention. She nodded again to the driver who smiled and pointed in the direction of the big stone archway. He barked a reprimand at the touts. They pretended to take heed but then did a loop and followed.

Doing her best to ignore them she walked up the steps past a young girl in rags who cradled a very young baby. The dark, pleading glance tried to find Mel as she kept walking. The girl did a hand to mouth gesture with grubby fingers. Mel pushed forward. Another hand grabbed her sock. She shuddered at the feeble grip of a man with no legs on a wooden pallet. *Keep going, Mel, come on, you should be used to it by now.* She hustled and threaded her way into the enormous main hall, a fading monument to the Brits.

Melissa hugged herself internally, feeling marginally safe in the entrance to a great hall. She was further relieved when the touts disappeared suddenly after saying no to them several times. Over in the corner a policeman in a khaki uniform smiled and gave a friendly salute. No doubt his presence made them honest.

Two hours to get a ticket to Kochi? How hard could that be, eh? No worries, Mel. At least it'd be nothing like trying to organise a mobile phone! She smiled. *Glad I didn't bother with that in the end. It would have taken all bloody day.* Last night she had spoken to Barry on the hotel phone and he was meeting her at the Kochi station down in Kerala when the train rolled in at about six the next morning.

She looked up at the huge fans inside the dome slowly whooshing almost in time with the echoing sound of people and luggage. Loudspeaker announcements bounced off the walls and peppered the humid air. The distant rumble of big diesels and the clank of heavy steel filtered in from the platforms. People filled the area, a sea of traditional dress, men mainly in white, women in bright colours and the black of Islam. All in a casual way with the balance of western fashions. They stood, sat on seats or on the hard granite floor. Some lay down, some slept, some ate, but most talked and yelled. Children ran around and played, beggars did the rounds and porters and officials moved around trying to look busy. Another policeman with a lathi strutted around proudly and reprimanded undesirables. Food and drink vendors rang bells and yelled sweet treats for sale, boys walked around with trays of marigolds. The scent of flowers, diesel, incense, and humanity hung in the wet air.

Mel grunted and sweated her way through the crowd and past the ammonia reeking toilets. She jumped at a gentle touch on the top of her right thigh. By the time she turned, lumbered with the rucksack, there were just dark faces and eyes, some challenging. It could have been any of them.

"Bastards," she mumbled and did a Military Two Step past a peanut wallah into the *Ticketings Office*.

The office was much smaller than the main hall but no quieter. She scanned the eight windows. Only three were open. Two lines of a dozen or more people zigzagged from the open grilles that seemed to protect two smartly dressed young men. The other window was labelled, *Disabled Passengers Only* where an overweight woman in a bright sari yelled at people through an open door behind. The only patrons in that line were a fat pi-dog with a litter of squeaking, feeding puppies. Mel glanced up at a sign on the wall, *Streamlined Computer Ticketing is now available here. Enquiries at the Information and Complaints Counter. By order, Government of India.* She looked at the *Information and Complaints Counter* - closed.

Melissa had plenty of time, at least an hour and a half before the Malabar Express departed on its way down the east coast of India. Barry had suggested that she get the hotel to arrange the ticket for her. *How hard could it be to organise a ticket?*

A young tout, with a bumfluff moustache, stood close to her. "I get ticket for you?"

"No thank you," she replied.

"Fast service, madam."

She forced a smile. "No thanks, I'm okay, really."

"But plenty of waiting. I am getting ticket for you, no charge, please sitting down on seat over there." He pointed.

She dropped the smile. "No thanks, mate, I'm okay."

She figured if she gave him money, he might take off with it or the ticket. As she wriggled the rucksack off, he tried to help. "Please, I'm alright." Maybe he was genuine? Hard to tell. It was annoying anyway. Mel glared at him.

"No problem, no problem." He stole another look at her breasts and disappeared.

Trains and carriages drummed, screeched, and clanked in the distance. Information from the loudspeakers ricocheted off the surfaces. Mel was confident everything would work out alright. The announcements crackled out in the local language at ear-splitting volume but sometimes so soft as to be indecipherable. Luckily for her, it was always repeated in English. Sometimes it was difficult to decipher but she felt confident of being able to find the right platform when the time came.

Melissa joined the shortest line behind a man in white kurta pyjamas. *Over an hour to go. Tons of time. Look around, Mel, enjoy being here.*

When it was the front person's turn to be served, several other people appeared from the greater nowhere and formed a babbling knot at the counter with the ticket seller. A Sikh in a light blue turban stood behind her and two Muslim women in black traditional dress ambled in behind him. All too close for her liking in the stifling heat. The overhead fans did not seem to make much difference. The line was a slow, depressing shuffle. The smell of body odour and curry tickled her nostrils. At various times she felt male gaze on her. *Why did I wear shorts?* She stared back at them but they did not avert their gaze. She glanced up at the big Roman clock on the wall.

Just under an hour to go, still plenty of time.

Now only one person was in front of her. A railway official came in and bellowed at a woman who squatted in the corner cooking something on a small gas bottle. Then he shooed the pi-dog and puppies away. The women behind continued to talk. *Almost there.* Her left foot continued the Saint Vitus dance.

Forty minutes to go. Her turn. "Umm, one first-class sleeper to Kochi, please."

She thought the din in the room dropped.

"Oh, I am sorry, madam, this line is only for second class passengers only." The young man moved his head gently and smiled not unkindly. "I do not have the facilities to be selling you a ticket."

"W-why?"

The Sikh in the blue turban stepped forward and pointed to the ground at her feet. A barely readable chalky painted sign said, **Second-class only**. Some Indian writing was also there, trampled and made grubby by thousands of feet.

"Can you …?" *How the hell was I supposed to see that!*

"No, madam. This is for Indian nationals only. Sorry, that line over there." He pointed and glanced over her shoulder. He did not need to say, "Next."

Mel squeezed her eyes shut, sighed as silently as her emotions would allow and dragged her rucksack over to that line. She was aware of the many eyes on her. By squinting she could now see the chalky scribble below the window on the floor at the head of her line. It was hard to read but she could at least decipher key words, **First Class**. Fortunately, there were only eight people in the line.

Thirty minutes to scheduled departure time.

She felt the tropical noise level return to normal. The fans continued to whirr and seemed to force down mouldy air from the domed ceiling. The line shuffled on. A fat, smelly man behind in a chequered table cloth lungi, tried to rub himself against her. *Pig.* She glared at him and put her rucksack between them. An announcement came over the loudspeakers. She could make out the words Malabar Express, platform 32. *Hell, the furthest platform. It'll be alright, take it easy, Mel.*

Ten minutes to go. Two people in front of her. Her heart pulsed and a throbbing had begun in her head. Sweat ran down her back. The two people in front both went to the counter together. It was Mel's turn next. There seem to be a disagreement, she could not really tell because they were speaking an Indian language. It was taking too long.

Hell, how bloody hard should it be to get a ticket? Five minutes to go. She badly needed a wee. The final call announcement over the loudspeakers bounced off all the surfaces. *How am I going to get in touch with Barry? I don't even know where he is staying. Come-bloody-well-on!*

The disagreement in front ended with head movements and barked words. Her turn. Her clothes were wet. Sweat dripped in her eyes and stung.

"Yes madam?"

What sort of idiot do I look like, buying a ticket for a train that has already probably left?

"Umm, could I please have one first-class sleeper ticket …" She looked up the clock. *Bloody Hell!* "One first-class sleeper ticket to Kochi … for tomorrow, please."

Dark eyes tracked Melissa as she staggered and stumbled past the now open **Information and Complaints** counter and out of the **Ticketings Office**. She then realised the experience of the last hour was nothing compared to the task of finding accommodation again as there was a local festival starting today. There were no vacancies at the place she had just come from. Also looming was the nightmare of somehow finding a way to contact Barry, a lifetime away.

The end

Life throws us challenges

Learn on the way

And make friends

BOUNCE

"Hey Lenny, stop throwin' the ball against the wall, would ya?" bellowed his mother from deep inside the house. "I can't hear the Jimmy Hannan Show."

"I'm gunna run away," he mumbled, throwing the ball again.

"Hey Lenny, jew hear what I said?"

"Yeah, righto Mum."

"What? Can't hear ya!" she yelled, "Hadta turn the TV down."

Lenny did a twinkle with two dirty fingers on his bottom lip. "Blah blah blah." He then turned and threw the ball again, hard. "Aaaah! No! Cripes."

The ball bounced, hit the roof of the FX Holden, rolled along the top of the trellis and into Kelvin Allen's place next door. He climbed onto the bottom rail and poked his head over the fence. "G'day Kel."

"Garn. Just got home from school, didn't see you at the bus stop."

"Nope, missed the bus. Mum an' Dad were arguing." He was not keen to talk about any of that, including the fact he did not have any clean clothes either. He shooed a fly away from his face.

"Coulda walked." Kel looked on, jug ears sticking out like butterfly wings.

"Yeah, s'pose. Me ball's over there. Hey Kel, gunna play cricket with me?"

"Guess so, probly not for long though, we have to go out to Aunty Melda's for tea. Wish I didn't have to go but."

"Yeah?"

Two magpies skipped along the fence.

"She always ruffles me hair and says how much I look like Dad."

"That all?" Lenny manoeuvred his skinny legs over the vertical corrugated iron fence. "Jeepers this tin's sharp, nearly cut me dick off."

"You shoulda climbed over near the chook house where the forty-four is, it's easier," said Kel, scratching his straw crew-cut.

"I know."

"Yeah, tennyrate and Aunty Melda always says what a good boy I am and if I study and read books, I'll be able to go to high school. Books are for girls. How old are you?"

"You know, I'm twelve. I got high school next year, that's if I pass. Anyway, got ya bat? You can bat if ya wanna." He ran a dirty hand through his brown prickly hair.

"Beaudy!"

"Here goes. Howz that!" yelled Lenny, first ball. Royce, the next-door neighbour's blue heeler burst into yelping and going nuts.

"Not out! Cripes Lenny, ya hit me in the guts, not the legs."

Kel batted himself in. "Gotta get the shine off the ball to make it easier for the next batsmen."

"That's stupid," chuckled Lenny. "We only got a tennis ball."

Kel burped. Royce continued to go crackers, scooting up and down the fence, yelping. "Royce, it's alright, come on mate. Bugger, you got him goin' now, Lenny."

"Kelvin, come inside, love, you've got to get ready to go out." Mrs Allen stuck her head out the side of the fly wire door. "Ah, g'day Lenny, how are you?"

"Not too bad thanks, Mrs Allen."

"That's the way, Lenny, that's the way. Kelvin's got to go out you know."

"Hey Mum, Lenny hasn't batted yet."

"All right. Five minutes, no more." They swapped positions.

"Here, Lenny, watch out for me googly. I'm Richie Benaud."

Lenny thought quickly. "My old man says I hold the bat just like Don Bradman. Anyrate, you wouldn't know what a googly was."

"Wanna bet? Dad reckons when I turn eleven, he'll let me play junior cricket." He concentrated through his sea of freckles, tongue sticking out like a cigar. "Right, watch out."

Smack! Lenny smashed the ball straight back into the fence. Royce went berserk again. "That'll learn ya," he yelled above Royce's frenzied yelps. "Dad says someone should chuck Royce a roast chook over the fence - with powdered glass in it an' soaked in arsenic. Reckoned that'd fix him."

Kel laughed loudly. "Right, smart arse. Last ball didn't get the spin right. Now this is the one. Watch out!"

"Take that. Ooooh cripes!" yelled Lenny as the ball sailed into Royce's yard. "That'll be the end of the ball, Royce rips 'em to bits."

"Kel?" His mum from inside.

"Gotta go, Lenny."

"Oh heck, Kel, how'm I gunna get me ball back?"

"Just jump over and get it. Umm, sorry ... er ... Lenny? Godda go ... er ... Royce wouldn't hurt a fly."

"Pig's bum he wouldn't. Remember that time we wuz ..."

"Hey boys?" A stiff grown-up voice rolled over the fence.

"Hey Kel?" whispered Lenny, grinning, "Sounds like Royce's dad."

"Naah, don't be a drip. It's Royce's master, not his dad." A bit louder. "Er ... yes, Mr Claymore?" The two boys stood on top of the compost bin and poked their heads over the fence. Kel continued. "Sorry, Mr Claymore, we accidentally hit the blinkin' ball ..."

"That's all right, lads." The old man leant back and hitched up badly pressed strides over a stretched striped shirt struggling with a beer gut. A fag end hung on his bottom lip like a wet worm. "If it happens again, you have my permission to jump over and get it. I have to go out soon. Don't worry about Royce, he wouldn't hurt a fly, would you Roycie? Now drop the ball, Royce. Come on boy drop the ball, that's a good dog."

Yellow eyes, mental dog. The old man picked up the ball and handed it to Kel. It was all gooey. Royce cranked up again, launched himself at the fence several times and zipped over to the other corner, then bounded up and down the fence with ear piercing yowls.

Kel looked at the saliva dripping through his fingers and said, "Um … thanks Mr Claymore." The old man nodded and wandered away.

"Quick, one more over," whispered Lenny.

"Let's go. How about this?" Kel bowled a quicker ball and it went straight through Lenny's stick legs and hit the rubbish bin wicket. "Howz that?" he shrieked.

"That's not fair; the ball hit a lump in the lawn."

"Kelvin, I won't call you again." Mrs Allen scraped food into the cat's dish just outside the back door.

"Yes mum, be right there."

"Bowl one more, quick," yelled Lenny.

"Get this … oh … no … heck! Crumbs," gasped Kel. The ball went flying over into Royce's yard again. "Look, I've gotta go."

Lenny watched his mate disappear inside the back door. "Bugger."

He climbed up on the compost bin and looked over. Royce catapulted up and down the fence and made distressed noises around the ball firmly in his mouth. "Mr Claymore? Mr Claymore?" Lenny tried a couple more times. It seemed Mr Claymore had already gone out. "Here boy, drop the ball."

It was clear Royce was not going to drop the ball; also, Lenny was not going to climb over and take the ball away from a dog as bonkers as Royce. He had an idea, glancing towards the cat's bowl at the back door. "This'd better work," he mumbled, tongue sticking out of the side of his mouth. He climbed up the fence again and flung a small piece of meat in front of the dog. Royce dropped the ball on the bottom rail of the fence.

"Good dog." Lenny could not believe his fortune. He threw the remainder of the meat as far as he could towards the other side of the yard. Royce went crackers again, and took off like a goanna, yelping and barking. Lenny quickly grabbed a stick and rolled the ball along the rail, hard to do on the other side of the fence between bits of tin, chook wire and wood. He jerked his hand in a gap between the palings but scratched his arm on a nail. "Ahhh, crikey!" The ball continued its journey and dribbled into the property at the back of Mr Claymore's yard. Royce continued the din and catapulted himself down the side and across the back of the house.

"At least they don't have a dog," winced Lenny licking the blood off his arm as he looked through the palings and wire at the torn, gooey tennis ball lying in Harrington's place. A crow in the gum tree out the front cawed a signal to another crow on the next ridge.

Lenny climbed over.

"It's alright, you can come in here." A faint whisper.

He looked up. It took a couple of moments for him to see her. The cubby house was a couple of branches up in the tree and very well camouflaged.

"Er … umm." Lenny was not very good with girls.

"Hey, Lenny, wanna come up and have tea with me?" whispered Claudia again.

"Tea? Tea … er …" he picked up the ball and threw it against the fence to get the goo off. "I don't really like …"

"No, silly, it's really cordial, not real tea, but I pretend it is like having a real cup, you know, like the grown-ups do. The rope ladder is on the other side of the tree. Dad made it for me. Mum said it was unladylike for girls to climb trees, particularly with dresses on. Dad said, 'What the heck'."

Lenny was not too keen on getting lumbered with a sheila. His Dad had told him, 'Sheilas are nothing but strife, son'.

"I've got some chocolate, too. Come on up."

That did it.

"Orright then but not for long." The rope ladder was just ordinary hemp with knots in it. He struggled, puffed, and panted; trying to make it seem like was no effort at all.

"See, that wasn't that hard, was it?" wooed Claudia with a smile and flittering eyelashes.

"Nah, really easy, hardly had to try, it was a real snack." Lenny rubbed his chafed hands trying not to let her see the red spots on his legs as well.

"Here, have a cup of tea." She poured two cups, little finger curled. "It's only cordial, but when I get older mum says it will be all right for me to have real tea. Far as I am concerned, I'm old enough now. Did you know that I'm twelve?" Lenny doubted that. Claudia did not wait for an answer. "Lime cordial isn't quite so bad anyway. Mum says tea has caffeine and tannin in it, says it's bad for growing bodies." She delicately put the cup to her lips. "Mmmmmmmm ... bee-oo-tiffool."

Lenny took a sip. "Er ... tastes orright, s'pose." He realised he was quite thirsty.

"More?" she said in an exaggerated dreamy way and then took a big breath. Lenny could not take his eyes off her budding breasts trying to push out from beneath the fabric of her flowery top. She filled his cup again. "What are you looking at?" She tilted her head and swept long black hair over her shoulder.

"What? Um? Yeah ... nothin'." He did not really know why or what. There was a need to change the subject though. "Er ... hey, did you build this cubby house yourself?"

"Yep, certainly did although Dad did help me a bit by passing up the pieces of heavy wood." She fiddled with a string of shells hanging above her. "How old are you?"

"Er ... um ... I'm thirteen." He sat up straighter.

"You don't look thirteen." She turned her head and shot him a school teacher look.

"Well, I am thirteen."

She lifted her head slightly and looked down her nose. "Anyway, what are you going to be when you grow up?"

"Well, I'm good at drawing but mum says only la-de-da boys do that. Dad's a truck driver; he says he doesn't want me to do drawin' or drivin'. Bastard of a life by two, he reckons."

"That's swearing. Swearing isn't polite, but Mum says some people can't help it. I'm going to be a fire-fighter. Some people call them firemen but girls can do it too, really well."

Lenny had to think quickly. "Yeah, I suppose I'll just have to be a soldier. They carry guns." He thought he was on the cusp of being good with girls.

"Guns are dangerous," she said. "Chocolate? The wrappers are almost the same colour as the red roses on my dress. Do you like my dress?" She took a deep breath.

"Yep." He stole a glance at her chest, grabbed the chocolate and quickly looked away. He knew the chocolate would not affect his dinner 'cos there would be none. Mum would be too drunk and Dad would get really mad because he'd have to make toast and soup for them all later on.

Mrs Harrington soprano'ed out the back window. "Claudia? Clorrr-deee-arrrrrre! Time for dinner, your father's just walked in."

"I've got to go." She lifted the hem on her dress, pretending to brush something off.

He took his time looking away. "Er … yeah, I s'pose I'd better go too."

"You go down first, then I'll show you the easy way, like the fire-fighters do. Did I tell you I'm going to be a fire-fighter, one day?"

"Yeah." He went to the rope, sliding down was easier, but his hands fizzed a bit as the rope had its revenge.

"You're getting the hang of it but you probably need more practice. This is how it's done."

She slid down the rope, all elegance and grace. He looked up her dress, his gaze zeroed in on her light pink underpants.

"See? That's how it's done. We must take tea again some time, eh?"

"Yep, sss'pose." He picked up the ball to hide the stammer. "Ball's still got goo all over it." He threw it hard towards the back fence. "Oh, bugger." It bounced over.

"Ummmmmmmmm, you swore again. Maybe you're one of those people who can't help it."

"Naah I only swear when there is a need to. Dad says that's all right."

Mrs Harrington's solo opera interrupted. "Claudia? Claudeeeeee aaaaarh! In here this instant. I won't say it again."

"Gotta go. Bye," she pouted a breath and skipped away.

Lenny heard her chuckling all the way to the back door. He had a slight swagger in his step. He was getting good with girls and looking up her dress made him feel strange inside and it was good.

He ran a wet tongue all the way around his lips as he climbed the fence into Aaron Ruthenbeck's place. Aaron had a dog too, but Lenny knew him pretty well.

"G'day Mandrake," coo-ed Lenny climbing down.

Mandrake the wonder dog waddled over with the ball in his mouth.

"Here boy, just drop it." The old dog dropped the ball, looked up and wagged his tail slowly. "Good dog," soothed Lenny as he picked up the ball. "Cripes Mandrake, it's got plenty of goo on it, hasn't it?" The old black Labrador wagged his tail even more. Lenny threw the ball hard against the other side fence. The dog slowly waddled after it.

Lenny heard spanner tinkering noises coming from the open door of the shed.

Aaron looked up, black oily hair hanging over his dark eyes. "Aaaaaah! G'day Lenny. What are you bloody well doing over here?"

"Ball came over the fence. What are you doing?"

"Fixin' me bloody bike, mate," said Aaron rubbing his oily hands on an equally oily rag. "Replacing the bloody piston. Have to have it ready for Dad so'ze he can ride it in the bloody scramble on Saturday. Wanna come?"

Aaron had taken Lenny along to the motor bike scrambles several times before.

"Yeah, wouldn't mind, although I don't know what I'm doing. Dad was supposed to be taking us to the beach Saturday, if the weather's alright."

"No worries, mate. If you don't make it this Satdee there's always next bloody fortnight. I'll be sixteen next bloody month so then I'll be arba da ride it meself." He ran both hands through his long hair, keeping the grease up. "The old man said I can smoke fags too when I turn sixteen. By the way, Lenny how old're ya?"

Lenny looked away for a second. "I'm ... um ... thirteen." Worth a try.

"That's bull," laughed Aaron, looking down his skeg of a nose. "You're only bloody eleven, aren't ya?"

"I am not! I'm thirteen."

Aaron looked at him and smiled again.

"Orright then, I am twelve, but I'm nearly thirteen."

"Fair enough. Anyrate, mind handing me that bloody spanner? No, the B S F one, yeah, that's it."

"Suppose I'd better be going," said Lenny, "Godda retrieve me ball from Mandrake."

"Yeah, rightoh. Mandrake is liable to hide the bloody ball, did you know he is a magician?" Aaron looked up. "Get it? Mandrake the Magician. That's how the bloody dog got his name."

Lenny did get it; his Dad always had the weekend paper with the comic strip. "Yeah. Ya toll me that once before. All right Aaron, see ya later."

He went down the back looking for the ball and called gently, "Mandrake? Mandrake? Oh, there you are."

The dog lay under the lemon tree gnawing on the ball. Old rheumy eyes defied, pleaded and played.

"Aaaare! Gawd. Here boy, gimmee the ball." Even though the dog was old, he still liked to play games and was reluctant to give the ball up. He gave a puppy growl and ambled behind the tree. "Come on Mandrake, give me the ball, orright?"

Lenny had an idea, not much of an idea but worth a go. He scratched his head, not sure why he even wanted the ball because it was shredded and mauled. He picked up an old dry bone, lying under the clothesline. "Here Mandrake, here boy, have this." Mandrake looked at him, looked at the bone, looked at him again, dropped the ball and waddled over to Lenny. "Good dog." Lenny patted his old head and gave him the bone.

Lenny picked up the wet, shredded tennis ball and chucked it hard against the fence.

"Aaaah! Jeepers! Not again." The ball dislodged a paling and disappeared into the Rossellini's back yard. He looked back, Mandrake stood there, tail slowly fanning, bone in his mouth, happy in the land of dog dementia. Lenny wiped his dirty hands on the lawn.

The palings were nailed to the timber rails from the other side so he could climb. He hoped Mrs Rossellini was not in the garden. He did not mind her, she was really friendly, always gave him some vegetables and eggs whenever she saw him or his mum or dad over the fence. Trouble was, he could not understand her because his Dad said she talked one of those dago languages. She was always dressed in black, too. The younger Mrs Rossellini went out to work as a cleaner at the abattoirs and was not there very much. He knew some of the other Rossellini's but not all and they went to another school. Others were grown up and visited now and then. His Dad told him their whole property was knee deep and almost alive with them because they were Catholics. Lenny vaguely knew Elanora, the youngest of the daughters.

Lenny spied the ball just over near the chook house. He easily climbed to the top of the fence but had to jump to the other side. He landed in the mulch and made his way under the grapevine, past the citrus trees to the chook house.

"What are you doing here?" Elanora frowned and held up her doll. "Miss Barbarella didn't hear you, but I did."

"Err ... umm ... yeah." Being good with girls deserted him for a moment. Then he realised Ellie was only very young. "Me ball bounced over the fence, see? Over there!" He pointed.

She giggled. "It's alright, Lenny, Nona says you are a well-mannered boy, not like those people on the other side. They stay up late and have bad women too."

Lenny relaxed a little. "Look I'll get the ball, if that's all right and head ..."

"No need to go," she commanded in a grown-up voice, "I'll put Miss Barbarella on top of her throne. It's really a bucket, you know. She stays in the background, never says much. Do you want a plum?"

"Plum?"

She chewed a blond pigtail. "Yes, we have plenty, and Nona would want me to offer you one. Here, sit down." The bench was a hardwood sleeper between two oil drums.

"Yeah, s'pose."

She lifted a tea towel off a bucket containing deep maroon plums. "There, please help yourself. Nona, did you know Grandma's name is Nona? Well, she makes jam and preserves all different fruits as well."

Lenny looked at his feet; he was in a cave for a second.

"It's alright, they've been washed," she said, giggling.

"Um ... thanks." What his Dad said about sheilas was probably true but Ellie didn't seem too bad. Dad reckoned they were a lot worse than blokes.

"Did you know that my family is from Italy? Most Italians have black hair but we're from the south of Naples and we are quite fair. People down there have black hair as well, you know."

"Umm ... yeah."

"I will be eight soon, too. Nona says that is almost grown up." She picked up her doll. "Barbarella is from Sicily, she has dark hair, and see? Her skin is dark, like mine. Do you know where Sicily is? Have another plum if you like."

"Er ... yeah."

"Is your Mother still having problems?"

"What?" Lenny looked at her, eyebrows straight lining. Too many questions.

"Nona says she is such a nice girl, but she has some sort of drinking attachment. What does that mean?" She did not wait for an answer. "Is she alright? We hear a lot of loud talking coming from your place."

"What? Yes ... no ...." Maybe he was not really that good with girls after all. "Er ... sometimes things aren't too good." Why was he talking like this, especially to a girl?

"I'll give you some things from the garden to take with you. Nona would like that. She says your Mum probably needs some good food."

Lenny's fingers fiddled. "Sometimes I think I'm gunna leave home, you know, just go somewhere else."

"Well, I can't go with you now because I'm only seven but when I turn eight, we could maybe go away for a trip. I don't think Mamma or Pappa would mind so long as it wasn't far. Anyway, I have to go on holidays to Wallaroo first. Do you want to come?"

"Er ... um ... no, I mean yes, but no I can't, Mum needs me I think, so does Dad. I better go."

"Anyway, Miss Barbarella needs to be fed I suppose. Please talk to her; I'll be back in a moment."

She jumped up and skipped over to the shed. Just as Lenny was about to get up, she struggled back with a cardboard box full of produce. "Here, you'll like the punkin, Butternuck, Nona says it's her favourite."

"Um … thanks, I'd better be going."

"You'll have to help lift the box on to the top of the fence 'cos it's a bit heavy for me," she puffed. "Oh, I wish I was eight. How old are you?" Ellie dragged an oil drum over to the fence and climbed up. She picked up the box again, grunting. He stepped over quickly and helped her lift it.

He puffed out his chest, "Thirteen. There. We can rest it on the top and I'll climb over, see? Easy, no worries. Ooooops! Nearly lost it. Um … er thanks Ellie."

"That's all right, maybe we can run away together in a few months." She giggled and made a moustache of her pig tail.

He climbed down the other side and grabbed the box.

"Forgot your ball," she chuckled through the slats and threw it over.

"Thanks, Ellie, again, um … thanks."

He heard her faint giggling as she disappeared into the grape vines.

Lenny put the box on the back step and went and retrieved the ball. He threw the ragged, gooey ball against the side of the house.

"Lenny! What the bloody hell are ya doing, orright? I thought I toll ya ta stop doin' that! I can't hear the bloody TV!"

He knew his Mum was getting worse because she was starting to swear.

"Yep, alright Mum," he shouted. He threw the ball again and mumbled, "I'm gunna run away, and soon."

Lenny knew tonight was going to be just as bad as every other night. Dad would come home, there'd be no dinner, the arguments would start. Then it occurred to him that he could have a go at cooking something. There was a box of stuff on the back step.

The end

Give the one you love

Flowers and April showers

Check the calendar first

APRIL FOOL

George was determined not to let her get him like the previous year.

Alicia really got me a good one alright, he recalled, jaw tightening. She had asked him to pop into the office supplies place and pick up a small parcel. The order was in a sealed envelope and there was no need to ask her what it was, nor look inside. She had told him that they rang her the night before, and she did not have time to collect it for a couple of days. Yep, no worries, of course he could fit that in for her. He remembered it well.

Finding a park in town was never easy and he was abused by a cliff hanging, unwashed, rust-bucket driver he had beaten for a tight spot. He had to walk away from the victimized human, who continued to radiate heated verbal abuse in his direction; then he had to stand at the front counter of the office supplies place, whilst a bloke with a comb-over pretended to be busy.

Time dribbled by, entertained by mindless commercial radio. Comb-over had to look up sooner or later.

"Er ... you right there, mate?"

George was angry enough to say, "Yeah, I love standing here like a stale bottle of piss waiting for a clown like you to condescend to do what you are bloody-well paid for."

He strangled that, knowing it was as pointless as wanting to speak to a real person on a 1300 number; so he rattled off the usual reply for these situations which happened all too often as far as he was concerned. "I'll never be alright, mate." George gathered strength. "Anyway, look, I've come to pick up a parcel."

He handed over the envelope. The man, who emitted the impression that nothing would get in the way of his imitation gold watch, grunted in concentration. Then a smirk straddled a smile. He looked up and started laughing.

"Someone's having a lend of ya, mate. The last batch of striped ink sold out last April Fools' Day."

George's head went into lights and colours. Close to boil. All he could manage was, "Fuck'n what?"

Comb-over's laugh diminished a bit, "No need to take it out on me mate, just 'cos you got, kind of, you know … got taken."

George spun on his heel and stormed out with the muffled laughter and talk-back radio following him like a fluff in a tracksuit. Striped ink? What sort of bean-head did he look like? Oh yeah, there was a driving need to get her back this year alright.

He collated a game plan in his head for Alicia and made sure he was up early on this particular day. Firstly, he jacked up the rear wheels of her car so she would think there was a broken axle when she tried to drive off. Then he sent her office an email saying Alicia had fallen in love with an artist and was going to Tuscany for a year to discover herself. The thought of filling her work bag with honey crossed his mind but he figured that might give the game away and spoil the reception she would get on arrival at work.

"This should do it," he sniggered as six sugars plopped into her morning cup of tea, "Just for starters, baby. This'll throw you off track."

George reasoned she would think that was probably all he was going to do and therefore she would not be ready for the other things to come.

"Cuppa, dear?" he bubbled, almost dancing into the bedroom like an upmarket waiter.

Alicia yawned, tousled her hair, and pulled herself up. He helped her and added an extra pillow. He had to admit that feeling up a woman, even though it was his wife, early in the morning, was not altogether bad.

"Yukkkkk!" she yelped. "George, what the hell is this, you know I don't have sugar?"

"April Fool!" he triumphed. "Got you there, didn't I?" He smiled the confidence of a re-elected politician.

"April Fool? You're the fool George, it's only the 31st of March today, not the first of April, you moron."

The end

No one owns sadness

Love is sometimes hard to see

Give others a chance

END OF STORM

Nine raindrops skidded across the bus window. Before the last stop there were only six.

"I hate this rainy weather," mumbled Haylee.

"Oh, it's not so bad, I mean, like, we only get a couple of months of it." Shauna leaned over and looked out.

"Yeah, I guess."

"Umm, by the way, how did you go in that literary competition, you know, your short story?"

"Well, I … I won the senior section."

"No way. Wow! That's great!"

"Yeah, I guess."

Shauna lifted an eyebrow. "Why so glum?"

"Nothin' really."

"Come on babe, it's Shauna, remember?"

"Oh well, it's dad's new girlfriend, Natalie. Like, don't do this, don't do that, do this, do that, heaps annoying."

"She can't be that bad, can she?"

"You better believe it. Dad let her move in and be, you know, mum."

"Aaaah, yeah, I know, must be tough. Ooooops, nearly missed my stop. Got to go, Hay. See you on the bus tomorrow. Bye!"

"Right, see ya."

She watched Shauna grapple her way down the lurching aisle. The bus stopped with a jerk. She flitted down the steps, gave a characteristic twinkle of her fingers, turned, and skipped off into the fizzing rain.

Haylee looked out the window. There were too many raindrops to count now, streaking across the window like an invading army. Winter cold seeped through her.

Natalie. Bitch. Well, no, not really. Maybe not, I'm not sure, she is probably just trying to please dad. She will never be my mum.

Even though it was only half past four, darkness pressed down on everything, reflecting how she was feeling.

She told her dad this morning about winning the competition. He was very happy. He hugged her and kissed her head. "I knew you would win; I just had a feeling; you are so good with your words. Your mother would have been proud of you." He choked on the last two words.

Natalie walked into the room tying her dressing-gown cord. "What was that?"

Haylee said, "Nothing." Dad came to her rescue and explained.

"That's wonderful Haylee," said Natalie and gave her a hug.

Haylee's response was as rigid as the word, "Nothing."

Yeah, sure. Natalie trying to take over again.

Hayley looked out the window. No more blobs, rain hit the window with spite and the darkness deepened. The bus lurched to a stop and Year 12 boys pushed and shoved each other down the aisle and tumbled off. Rain now pelted down.

If God cared, why did good people get cancer? Haylee remembered the day when her mother said, "Hay, I've got something to tell you." Her mother died two months later. Trying to be brave for herself was bad enough, but she needed to be there for her dad too, that was the hardest thing. Hayley watched her father try to cope without his beautiful wife, her mother.

Time heals, yeah sure. Her father met Natalie at the self-help group. Her husband had died of cancer too. Haylee was happy for her dad, but Natalie? She would never replace her mum.

The bus clanked and lurched twice and then stopped abruptly about 50 metres from her stop. The rain hammered down. It seemed like night-time. The cold penetrated. Haylee felt a pang of guilt for the way she had spoken to Natalie that morning.

"Ah drat!" barked the driver.

She might have missed her stop had it not been for the bus grinding to a halt. It was lucky because it had pulled up right opposite her corner. Haylee grabbed her things and made her way to the front. She was the only passenger.

The driver said, "Oh, sorry love, the bloody bus has conked out, lost electrics. Just wait a minute and I'll organise a taxi for ya. I've got to get the mechanic here anyway." He reached out for his mobile phone.

"Umm, that's okay," blurted Haylee, "I only live just up there." She pointed.

"Look, wait a tick. I can't let you go out in this!"

They looked out into the blinding rain. Street lights had come on. They both looked at each other.

She said, "It's fine, I only live just down there, this side of that rubbish bin, see?" She pointed again.

"I'd be neglecting my duty if I let you go out there." He picked up his mobile.

Just then the drum roll on the roof eased but the blustery squall swished against the windows.

"It's okay thanks, I'll dash."

He touched her arm. "Wait, you can use my umbrella. Just give it to the driver tomorrow, when you get on the bus. It will find its way back to me. Here."

She smiled, slightly embarrassed. "Umm thanks, I ..."

"That's okay, love, not a problem. I'll stand here on the step, and you can wave when you turn into your place, right?"

"Thanks, it's very ..."

"No worries, way you go, I'll keep an eye on ya."

Haylee slung the school bag over her shoulder as he popped the umbrella. She scooted off in the fizzing cold. She half turned and yelled thanks in the direction of the candlelit bus. Just as she reached her place, she turned squarely and waved. He gave an exaggerated salute and faded from view.

Haylee opened the gate. The dog barked and rushed to her.

"You're all wet, Brenton," she said, relieved to be home.

Someone must have heard the commotion, the door opened.

Natalie stood there holding up a small present or something in her hand. "I … er come in love, you must be soaked." She opened her arms ignoring the cold, wet clothes. Haylee felt the warmth.

Her father came over, put his arms around both of them and kissed the top of her head.

Haylee's legs went to jelly. She softened and started weeping.

The end

Promises

Should never be taken lightly -

Courage and love sit side by side

FINAL CARD

"Well dad, I'll drop in on you tomorrow afternoon. Jane said she'd call in before lunch." Dave stood and stretched.

"Can check out day after tomorrow. Doc seems to be happy enough with things - I don't feel too bad either."

Both laughed. They loosely clasped each other's hands.

The old man lifted one eyebrow. "Remember what I said, son?"

"No worries, dad, you've given me enduring power of attorney and all that. But, it's a long way off, before … you …"

"Yeah, you mean, die?"

"Don't worry, Dr Avery showed you the chart, you're in good health. It was just a minor operation, alright? Said your heart wasn't as strong as it could be, but dad, it's okay."

"Yeah, I guess so …"

Dave smiled. "Look dad, quit worrying. You're getting out of here, day after tomorrow, right?"

The old man sighed. "Suppose you're right. Be good to get back into playing cards again with Stan."

"Nothing wrong with you, ol' mate," said Dave at the door, giving a loose salute and a broad grin. See you tomorrow."

"Righto, son."

∞

The next afternoon Dave arrived at the ward with a small suitcase.

"How are you feeling, dad?" smiled Dave.

"Oh, not bad. Any mail?" replied the old man.

"Mail? Er … no dad." Dave had thought it through, he was not really lying. After all it was only an envelope that did not have a stamp. *So, not really mail.* He figured he could tell the old man when he got out. He would have to know; Dave knew that but now was not the time.

"Anyway, Doc says I can go home tomorrow morning. I sort of feel a bit weak, though."

"Oh, they'll take pretty good care of you at the village, dad. I had a chat to Mrs Wade; she says they miss you."

"Yeah, I know. Can't wait to get back there. Surprising, isn't it?"

"What? Why is that?"

"Well, remember when mum died? I didn't want to go to the village, but now, been there 10 years, like home. Got good friends there, you know. By the way, how's Stan?"

"Stan? Stan? Oh yeah, he sends his regards. Anyway, dad got to go."

They shook and caressed.

"She's a good girl, that Jane. Thank her for dropping in this morning, won't you?"

"Yep, no worries. Doc says they'll discharge you about ten in morning. I'll see you a bit earlier than that anyway. I'll put this case in the closet and we'll organise your gear tomorrow, okay?"

"Thanks son, you're a good boy. I wanted to tell you that."

Dave's colour rose and he glanced down. "Mmm … look dad, no worries …"

Dave left the hospital happy enough that his father was okay, alive, and well. For how long? Who knows? Dave was not that young himself. The weight of the envelope in his back pocket was troubling.

∞

The hospital car park was nearly full at nine thirty the next morning but he jagged a spot near the entrance. Stan's letter was addressed to his father. He knew he should not have opened it but there was something about the envelope. The flap was not sealed very well and dislodged when he grabbed it out of the old man's pigeon hole. Stan's name appeared on the back. Mrs Wade had informed him of Stan's death.

Dear Mike,

Recently I heard that I've got liver cancer. I'm getting to the stage where I can't look after myself, can barely make it to the dunny on my own. Pain is really bad, I can't go on. All I have is my dignity. Remember those purple pills I showed you that I'd been saving up? By the time you get this I'll be dead. Last card eh? I'm of sound mind and I know what I'm doing. I thought a letter was a better way to tell you.

Goodbye old friend, you have been a great mate.
Stan.

He looked through the windscreen, towards the tangle of diehard faggers at the entrance to the hospital, not really seeing anything. He focused again when he heard a far-off siren just as his mobile joined in.

"Dave here."

"Ah … mister, sorry, Dave? Doctor Avery here, I'm afraid the news isn't too bright …"

"Dad?" Dave jerked upright.

"Yes, I'm sorry. He had a stroke not long ago … I'm sorry."

"Is he … how …"

"It was a massive stroke; he's only just with us. Can you come in now?"

"I'm here, in the car park, yeah, see you in a minute."

Dave dodged and weaved through the mêlée at reception and dashed to the ward.

"This never gets any easier, Mister … look sorry, I mean Dave," said Dr Avery. "It was more than just a murmur in the scope of things, the stroke I mean. Prior to, all his vital signs were good, we didn't see it coming. We knew his heart wasn't as strong as it could have been, but … these things happen, his age was against him."

"I understand, doctor," mumbled Dave slowly shaking his head.

"Look, mate, we don't expect him to recover, he is being kept alive with oxygen, but his brain isn't functioning at all. Unfortunately, to tell the truth, he *will not* recover. It might be good if you sit with him a while and then we'll talk."

They went into the room; the doctor spoke softly to a nurse as he checked the tubes and gauges. "I have to finish my rounds, I'll drop back in about twenty," he said and quietly disappeared.

"Sit here," soothed the young female nurse, drawing a chair alongside the bed. "It's okay, just hold his hand. Please press this if there is any change in the monitors." She picked up a clipboard and swished out of the room. The door clicked.

"Dad, dad." Tears welled in his eyes as he stroked his father's hand. He thought he heard the old man speak. But he knew he did not.

Remember what we talked about, son? The old man lay still, eyes closed, chest rising and falling.

"Oh, dad," said Dave. *Not much of a life for the future.*

He kissed his father and then stroked the thinning, grey hair. He had difficulty seeing through the tears. All those things they talked about; being able to look after yourself, quality of life, most of his friends gone, being ready to let go. His hand hovered over the oxygen bottle for a long moment.

"Oh dad, I love you, old fella." Dave turned the oxygen tap. He knew he didn't have long.

The sound of the monitors squawked and beeped and then slowly the line went steady. With his eyes on the glass panel in the door, a few seconds later he opened the valve and pressed the button to summon help.

The end

Life is to enjoy

Try to embrace new things

Impending death becomes the comfort zone

A QUIET PLACE

I'm a bit of a yuppie. I don't mind admitting it. I don't think I'm better than everyone else, but you know ... anyway, but I'm certainly better off than a lot of those someone else's though.

We don't have kids to drain our finances, that's probably the main reason why we are members of the *haves* as opposed to the *have nots*.

Anyway, me and the missus, it's always me and the missus, decided to rent a unit up the coast for a few days. A nice quiet spot, somewhere where there weren't too many people, a place where they actively discourage kids or at least that's what someone told us. Not that we don't like kids, of course we do, well ....

We do, provided we don't have them staying at our place, don't have them for very long, don't have them for meal times and don't have them for nappy changing, or any of that stuff.

These are rules we try to stick by, but choice isn't always an option. Recently, some people we hadn't seen for some time rolled up a couple of hours before dinner. The missus had just got me a cuppa. I'd said, "Darl, it's good-oh having the whole day to ourselves, isn't it, eh?" Gawd struth, there they were on our doorstep.

So, we had to pretend we were thrilled to see them, which of course we were, but only in one sense. In another sense we were bloody well annoyed because they never rang.

They said, "Hope we haven't caught you at a bad moment. We were in the area and thought we'd *just* pop in. We wuz gunna ring but, you know … can't stay for long though." Those innocent sentences generally hide a multitude of lies like, *We are going to stay for dinner, too.*

In the short space of time it takes to utter those words, the kids were already going berserk using the lounge as a trampoline. Then the missus had to zip around in a panic, hunting for enough food to feed four extra people. Plus, enough food for the kids to play with and throw around. But fair enough, you are sort of glad to see them, but not their kids.

The drama unfolded as predicted, the kids completely ruled the afternoon. We didn't get a chance to relate to our friends at all because the nippers demanded so much attention. Climbing all over their parents, interrupting, yelling, and screaming, running around our formal lounge room whilst dropping food everywhere.

Finally, as if on cue, they asked if we had any raspberry cordial to give the kids. Any half-wit could see that would make them more unmanageable. The missus gently mentioned to these morons that this was probably counterproductive. They explained that there wasn't much they could do because the little tackers have hyperactive disorders and they didn't like anything else, unless we had Coke.

Then, you guessed it, the nappy fell off the little one and we ended up with poop all over our Afghani rugs. The parents laughed, funny as, and we kind of had to do the same; talk about cute, and dad inclined his head and said, "Kids. The little blighters have their moments but by jingoes I couldn't imagine life without 'em." Me and the missus could easily because our house stank like a lavvy.

They insisted on not stopping for dinner but they knew we would be obliged to ask so they stayed for dinner. We got through that with the kids throwing food and tantrums and eventually the mum said, "Well, must be going now, gee whiz, it's tremendous ta see yas again."

We pretended we were sorry to see them go but we didn't overdo it. So, after false starts at going they finally went, leaving enough food on the floor and walls to feed the homeless. Our next week was spent inadvertently sitting on rotten bananas or blobs of poo.

∞

Because of our busy lifestyle, short holidays are necessary so we decided on a few quiet days up the coast. Away we went in my late model four-wheel drive that has never engaged four-wheel-drive.

I've got the latest Pajero. That's the car yuppies drive. I have a key ring with a big Pajero insignia so people can see that I am a *have*. Someone told me that in Spanish it means wanker. I looked it up and they are wrong. I think it's just jealousy. I also wear Nike, not Dunlop Volleys.

The resort we decided on was a controversial plot of land a few years ago. Some idiot greenies reckoned it was inappropriate for development, but from what I'd seen on TV at the time it looked alright to me. Who needs all those rubbishy trees, swamp, sand flies and mozzies? After all, where would people like us go for holidays if there weren't resorts to go to, eh?

We arrived at our destination and went into the office to get our key and find out some local info. The sheila behind the counter wasn't a bad looking sort and her low-cut top gave me something to gawk at.

She smiled and said to us, "Here's your key and if you need anything else just pop over."

I tried to catch her eye but she played hard to get and it became clear she gave everyone the same line. Then she said, "Enjoy!"

I would and I knew she'd say, "Have a nice day." She did. How American can you get?

I waited for, "Missing you already." It wasn't forthcoming.

We found our unit easily and it had the potential for a nice aspect but we couldn't see the sea because there were bloody trees in the way. I thought I'd suggest to the management that they cut the damn things down. What's the point in being that close to the sea and not being able to see it? We also had a view of the neighbour's patio which was pretty ugly, although there was a bikini hanging on the line.

Quietness, at last.

"Ay luv, 'ow about a cuppa tea?" I yelled in the direction of my loving and attentive wife, who was the sort of sheila who was good in the kitchen when she wasn't watching TV. Just then a luxury clipper, commonly known as a bus, rolled up full of touros who swivelled their heads like clowns at the show.

"Oh no," I said as the big bus pulled up almost under our rear balcony. The bus driver made it clear that the engine would be running whilst the bus was parked, to keep the air-conditioning going. All sorts of elastic-necks scrambled off but the big diesel kept idling on, emitting choking light grey fumes straight up into our window. That might have seemed beaut to some people but wasn't worth a nugget of rocking-horse shit to me.

After the passengers jumped off, the coach captain sat on the bottom step of the bus. As if by mental telepathy he looked up in my direction. Our eyes met and he smiled, waved, and yelled, "Ow ya garn mite? She's real good out here, nice'n quiet too, eh, away from it all." He couldn't have thought it was smoky enough so he lit a cigarette.

I nodded and then under my breath I mumbled, "It was until you came along and spoilt it, you ignorant pin-head."

I kept smiling because being the driver of the big diesel, he couldn't possibly understand anyone who didn't eat, drink and sleep diesel. Also *had* he heard what I'd said, to live up to being the driver of a big diesel, and having a big tattoo on his forearm, he would have been obliged to climb up the balustrade and belt me right in the kisser. Diesel heads are like that. Simpletons.

I closed the door and went to the front of the unit. I could still hear and smell the big diesel but I figured everyone has to make allowances for moron-heads, even if they are lower socios. The missus handed me a lovely cuppa as I positioned myself in a cane chair, preparing to watch the touros getting away from it all. There seemed to be a lot of photo taking, babbling and yelling with the occasional scream thrown in by kids, who, don't get me going on it, in recent times have more rights than adults. One ignoramus in parachute shorts with his moon-headed boys headed off through the dunes, chucking litter as if they needed to leave a trail in case they became lost. Funny thing was, at least it was to me, he left the walkway at the sign saying,

Nature Reserve. Please keep to pathways. Area closed for regeneration.

Couldn't at least one of the stupid moron kids read? Still, I suppose he was getting away from it all, wasn't he? Bloody drongo.

The touros disappeared in all directions, probably on the warpath to leave their mark around the joint. Some were chucking live cigarette butts to promote fire in case the former didn't work. I didn't mind the idea of burning down the trees because I'd get a view. I just didn't want it to happen during my stay.

The diesel bus out the back kept idling over. It had been going for over an hour. I could never work that out. All truckies have a mental block about turning off the motor.

From the front of the unit, I had a view of the scrub and the sea was there in the distance. The missus was getting away from it all by watching TV. She did her best to turn it up for the ads, like most people do, even though the ads are louder anyway. I'm a person who doesn't watch TV, at least I'm not like most punters who watch TV almost every waking hour and claim to not to and also reckon the ads don't affect them. They're the ones who walk around singing ads and jingles. Boofheads. People must think the ads are much better than the programs. The companies spend more money on them and there are more ads than programs anyway. I mean with so many ads and idiot announcers going on about coming up, that story later, after the break and still to come. It's a wonder there is anything on other than ads. So, with ads bellowing, I decided on a walk down the beach because around the units it felt a bit like a grand final in a country town.

I strolled down to the harsh bright beach, dodging others as much as possible because I'm not much good with people. How funny is that, I'm a Human Relations Manager in the Public Service.

One of the touros, a bloke in a Mr Magoo gob hat with a T shirt that said, *Richard da Turd,* skinny white legs and a big fat gizzard hanging over some trying to be groovy board shorts, mumbled to me, "It's nice and peaceful 'ere mate, 'cept some inconsiderate guttersnipe has got their blasted TV up real loud, still ya get all types I s'pose."

He wandered off dropping a tissue, a film packet, and the plastic it came in, and flicking a lighted fag into the bush. If the fire took, I'd get my view. What a drip!

It was much more pleasant on the beach. The sea was a different blue than the sky. There were a few people enjoying themselves around the place so I took a long walk. The water looked pleasant but I couldn't face a swim. I am 55 years old and used to sitting in an office. My legs were a bit on the white side and I had a bit of girth, but basically my condition wasn't *too* bad. I decided to jog for a while but that only lasted a couple of minutes, so I reverted to a walk instead as that seemed more sensible. Then I sat down for a bit and had a bit of a perv on some young sheilas who happened to be nearby. My eyes zeroed in on them, couldn't help it, I'm a bloke.

After a while I went back to the units. It was nearly nice and quiet; the bus had gone but of course the TVs were going in most of the units ... tuned to different ads. I figured soon someone would stumble on the idea of making a video of ads. That would be a real hit! It would enable people to get away from it all and watch their favourite ads all day, every day, at will and not do anything else. I shelved the idea of doing it myself because I'm too gutless to do anything other than be a public servant; too keen on super and sick leave. I'm not a risk-taker.

It was about the time of day when I decided on a scotch. I poured myself a large one and offered the missus one as well but her concentration couldn't be penetrated as she was tuned into the ads. I should have known better than to speak to her during the ads. Waiting for the program to start was not necessarily better because I would have had a long wait.

I sat out the front and grabbed one of the 4WD magazines that I'd brought with me. I brought these mags in case someone should notice, because as a yuppie it was a necessary status symbol and to also project the belief that I had a few bob ... firstly to buy the mags and secondly to keep up to date with the latest four-wheel drives on the market.

Me and the missus are pretty comfortable. She's the same as me, a public servant, a physical education consultant manager with a behavioural science degree. But we have no kids so we're well off compared to most. Anyone with kids would agree with that. In fact, I don't think you could be a yuppie if you had kids, unless you were a CEO or perhaps your kids were grown up and were supporting themselves and not living at home. But not much chance of that, baby boomers have made a very hard bed to lie in there.

Gawd, everyone I know who has kids over 18, in fact any age, can't get rid of them! They're like dog crud in your ripple soles. You don't have to be Barry Jones to figure out that these people have spoilt their children so badly that the little blighters, and they're not really little after they get into their thirties, will *never leave home.*

This simpleton of a bloke I know told me recently, after he had to take an extra job stacking shelves at Coles from nine thirty at night to two a.m. to support his children, "You can't deny your kids." Funny thing was, well funny to me but obviously not to him, his kids were 26, 28 and get this, 31 years old! All three didn't work, had never worked, and obvious to me had no intention of working.

His wife looked ragged and sick after a cancer operation and had taken ironing on as well as her full-time job. They had not only worked their guts out to put their youngsters through school, but were working themselves sick to support these lazy, spoilt little shits to continue in that vein for the rest of their lives. He said to me, "When I got crook with depression, I asked them once to help out a bit around the house as they don't go to work like me and the wife, I mean they do it hard, believe me."

Pig's bum they do. "Did they?" I queried. His eldest probably gave him the finger and said, "Get a life Pop, ya silly old fart! Hey, can ya give me 50 bucks to buy drugs?"

"Well, they put the bin out." And my friend went on to say, "But they're mighty good kids, they brought home Hungry Jacks the other night – me an' mum didn't have to cook that night, they're good kids really. Hard yakka getting a job out there."

At the time I was about to say, "You stupid clown, you probably gave them money to buy the food anyway, *and*, they're not bloody kids *and*, as long as you keep spoiling them, they're never going to grow up, nor leave home. Why would they? Would you?"

But I didn't say it because he would no doubt regurgitate the usual weak-as-wee reply, "It's okay for you, you don't know what it's like to have kids, it's alright for you sitting in your position of judgment but it just isn't that simple! Not these days, kids 'ave got it tough, mate, and I mean really tough."

What a dope, even pretending to justify how weak he is.

∞

Anyrate, I sat on the patio in the semi-shade sipping scotch, reading a 4WD mag and watching the day disperse and thinking how good it was to be alive. Then my attention was diverted when a blonde sheila from the apartment next door ambled out and hung a towel over the rail. I pretended not to maul her with my stare but I did, like all blokes do, they can't help it, no more than *they* can help wearing sexy clothes. She arched her back, bent over and did all the things that sheilas do when blokes are around. Then she looked towards me, I nodded, she feigned minor surprise and then went back inside. I got a good free squiz at her bum wobbling inside a sarong.

Time for another scotch, not much else going on. The missus finally looked up and back at the TV just as quickly when I went in and I said, not in a demanding tone of course, "How about me dinner."

She replied without losing concentration or taking her eyes off the screen, she was a champion at it, "In a minute, dear, I just want to see this ad; it's a really good one."

I bit, I had to, "But hun you've seen it hundreds of times, why do you want to *just* see it again?"

"Oh, I dunno, it's just a good ad, that's all, dear."

So, I went and had a leak which presented an interesting challenge. I'd come across the same thing before at other resorts. The dunny seat was fitted in such a way that it wouldn't stay up. Which meant I had to keep one knee against the seat to hold it up whilst I had a wiss. During the process, of course, it went all over the shop. Maybe the person who designed this dunny was a woman who thought that blokes would then decide to sit down to wee instead of trying to hold the seat up. Most blokes I know would leave the seat down and leak all over it and everywhere else as well because most blokes I know never cleaned the dunny. It was women's work if ever there was. Also, most blokes wouldn't sit down to wee, or if they did, they certainly wouldn't tell anyone. Gawd, blokes and sheilas are funny in their own ways.

"By the way, where's me dinner?"

∞

The first night went well. Me and the missus had a normal night relaxing away from it all, she hardly said a word as she was watching TV and I was reading 4WD mags. Commercial TV hammered out mind numbing advertising in most of the units but when bedtime came, I was tired enough for it not to matter.

It was different the next morning however. At about 6:30 a.m. we were woken by some inconsiderate jerk with the TV on, and as well, shrieks and screams of joy from the pool. Evidently some kids decided to have a good time at the pool side. There were two young couples down there with their kids, getting away from it all. It was annoying that the young girls couldn't stop screaming and yelping. Maybe it was the chlorine, maybe it was the level of wee-wee in the water or the odd Bondi cigar that brought on sounds of hysteria. The young boys were much quieter but that was because they were piddling around with the filter system, right in front of their parents who, as could be predicted, didn't seem to give a root.

Just then a big new diesel Landcruiser pulled up, towing a huge runabout. Out jumped five kids and I must say a not bad looking red headed sheila. Even though it was early and I was cheesed off having my sleep pole-axed, I inadvertently made a comment on what she would look like without her top.

My wife rolled over, "What was that dear?"

"Nothing hun, just adjusting to another day in this place of quietness," I replied rubbing my eyes, and ears. She's a real sport, the missus. At least she doesn't have to put up with much from me, not like some blokes, and I make plenty of allowances for her.

After 20 minutes of backing and re-backing the driver finally placed the boat where he wanted it. It probably wasn't where the management would have liked it but I dare say the management probably wouldn't say anything to him because he was a huge, mean looking bastard with tats; secondly, he drove a diesel and by the look of the bikes and swimming aids and other possessions tied to the vehicle and boat, he felt very strongly about not denying his kids.

The pin-head parked the huge, expensive boat and his vehicle in such a way that no one could use the roadway very easily. Human nature on display I always say when a drip like this does something stupid but normal to them. Just as I knew he would; he left the big diesel idling away, filling our already noisy environment with grey diesel fumes and the rattle of a Landcruiser engine. Like all diesel engines, new or old, it needed new injectors. In addition to that, the not so bad looking red-head walked over near our balcony and started yelling at the kiddies 20 metres away.

All this at six forty-five in the morning! It was obvious we were in for a bottler of a day.

I felt like saying, "Hey, give the kids some cordial and lollies, why don't ya?" Bloody hell.

I closed up, made a cuppa for the missus. My job when on holidays but only brekky time though. Then I put together a bowl of cereal and milk to save her getting up to get it for me. I went out the front where it was much more relaxed although the birds made a fair bit of a din. They could have done with a bird scarer there in the morning. However, after five minutes, almost as if God had quickly contacted the gardener, an edge trimmer started up about five metres away. With the smell of two-stroke, freshly cut lawn and the whiff of sliced dog's dooty, I decided to go for a long walk on the beach by myself. The yawning missus had put a video on, even though it was early. She needed to relax for some reason, so she said, anyway.

When I had walked a couple of hundred metres an elderly couple walking towards me stopped. The old bloke said, "Ya won't catch no fish around here mate … there's nothin' around these days." The old lady rolled her eyes skyward. Their Jack Russell Terrier just looked at me and tried to wee on my leg and then tried to bite me when I kicked. They turned and walked away. The dog ran after them and they turned again and watched the dog squeeze out a nasty porridgey mess. No way they were going to pick that up, didn't even cover it with sand. At least the bloody dog didn't bite me. Irresponsible galahs.

I found a spot away from others. I put my towel over my gear and headed for the surf. The water was cold and my credentials jumped back into my guts, but I persevered. Just when I relaxed enough in the water, I noticed a couple wandering along the beach. Their two dogs were running ahead of them playing, yelping, and barking. I further noticed the dogs head towards my towel, so I wrangled out of the water to make it obvious to the couple that it was my towel and I didn't really want their dog territory stamped on it. The young couple didn't seem to give anything that resembled a stuff what their dogs did and it was obvious that one of the dogs was going to piss on my things.

Takes a bit to get me worked up. "Hey!" I yelled.

The couple looked at me as if I was the three-headed man from the circus. They strode off in a huff as I cursed the departing dogs.

Like I said, ball-tearer of a day, to complete my doggie lesson, on the way back through bush in front of the units, I was confronted by a Rottweiler. The bloody bastard of a thing just anchored and stared. My bottie nearly gave way. Before I could take evasive action, the owner, who must have been the owner because he looked just like a Rottweiler, as well as being obviously insecure and saddled with deep psychological problems, appeared, and gave the dog a command. "Oi!" he said.

What a cretin!

They continued past me to the beach, no doubt geared up to frighten the daylights out of others. It was clear the owner got a kick out of that sort of thing. I wanted to ask why he needed a wreckers' guard dog that's bred to kill. He probably would have said that little Adolf wouldn't hurt a fly. I could only hope that the Rottweiler would kill the other stupid dogs on the beach, the other owners would attack this insecure idiot and this insecure idiot would attack them. Alas, karma doesn't work like that. It seems to take longer, that's what I don't like about those eastern religions. As he walked past, he said, "It's a nice quiet place here buddy, pity about that inconsiderate person with the TV goin' full bore up there. Bloody loud eh." He gestured with a thumb.

The dog lifted its leg and leaked on the sign.

Strictly no dogs on beach.

A few minutes later I had settled back with a cuppa, that incidentally I had to get myself, as the missus was enveloped in general daytime TV ads. She did say she'd get my lunch just after an ad that she just wanted to see because it was a *really* good one. Anyway, I just settled down again when the gardener cranked up the ride-on mower and proceeded to mow the grass, even though there was very little lawn and it didn't need mowing. I was sure he was employed by God just to remind us that there is no paradise on earth. I sat there for a while and waved at the gardener sarcastically, giving him the finger when he wasn't watching.

He looked up, smiled, and bellowed, "Beaut quiet little spot she is 'ere mate, isn't she?"

I mumbled to myself, "You're a mental idiot, mate." After my experiences so far that day, it dawned on me that I should have used politically correct logic and considered myself the drongo. Blame myself because it was noisy as hell, blame myself because a dog wanted to piss on my towel, blame myself because a dog wanted to bite me, blame myself because I don't get a thrill out of diesels, or watching my dog do poo and the thrill of seeing someone tread in it.

Anyway, it wasn't all bad. The sheila next door came out again and took her tracksuit off, leaving a skimpy bikini. She caught me looking and feigned the minor outrage thing again. She went inside, came out again and lay on her towel at the other end of the balcony where she eased off her bikini top. I waited some time for the next stage but it didn't eventuate.

However, that pleasant interlude didn't last as the gardener finished mowing and started up a leaf blower, and then, Mister *I've got a big new car, a big new boat, me missus is a bit of a doll and I won't deny my children*, started up his boat motor. Initially, I was silly enough to think he was just doing a test run.

He had the motor running for some time, and I hoped, because it wasn't in water, it might seize up … but it didn't. After about ten minutes he switched it off. Then he looked up and noticed me, gave a stupid grin and yelled, "She's a beauty, isn't she mate? Bugger me, it's a great little spot this, nice'n quiet, eh?"

I wasn't too keen on buggering him, I felt like belting him but he was bigger than me. Then he turned and bellowed at his missus who was swearing at the kids as they proceeded to break limbs off shrubs and throw lolly wrappers all over the place. Bloody circus clowns.

Just then I heard from a distance away, **SCREECH! BASH! CRASH! BANG!** I wondered what could possibly make that much noise. Then a big purple truck, diesel of course, faulty muffler and billowing smoke, pulled up underneath our patio. **SCREECH! BASH! CRASH! BANG!** It was the Clean-it-Away truck collecting rubbish.

That took the biscuits, cake, savories, tray, and all! I had never heard anything as loud and as disturbing as that. I wasn't exactly frightened but I was certainly anxious, I could feel depression setting in. I needed my medication again.

I sped inside, closed all doors and windows, put the air-conditioner on and sat down in front of the TV. The ads didn't exactly soothe me, but it wasn't as loud as outside. I asked the missus to get my blood pressure tablets and a glass of water. She told me she would soon but there was a really good ad, one I should see, coming up after the break. All I could do was sigh.

The next few days I hid indoors. I didn't care that the resort was built on a controversial piece of land. All I had to look forward to was the weekend when we returned home. I was more than ready for work after our holiday. Next year I vowed to stay home and watch TV.

The end

Time to move up

For the wrong reasons

Escape is down to luck

RICOCHET

His confidence dropped like a sinker. New South Wales police officers, two of them, chequered peaked caps Gestapo style, leather jackets and boots, arms out like gunslingers. They glanced at him, level along the platform, and then at each other for a moment. Both turned and looked hard at him, then started the march in his direction. Echoes of footsteps and voices bounced off the tiles and tunnels. An electric train quaked the underground in the distance.

They kept coming, locking him in their line of sight. Sweat poured out of his beanie into his eyes and he could smell the halo of his bad breath.

Bevan knew it was all over. *Narelle, that bitch! Those public servants, and the rest of them … bastards.*

∞

Bevan was going to get it together. No more lining up at the employment office and pretending to look for work. *Go and be a landscape labourer in Port Kembla? Work on the roads at Gosford? Pick fruit at Shepparton? Pig's arse. They had to be joking! Those bastards, public servant mongrels, probably on 80 grand a year. It was easy for them to say, sitting in air-conditioned offices, typical overpaid arseholes.*

And the rest, politicians, bankers, and CEOs, all on the take. They were all at it. Why shouldn't he have some of it?

Bevan provided a service for people; he was an essential part of the community. He was definitely going to move up the chain of command. The proceeds had just come in from two *borrowed* cars and a wad of cash from a shed full of power tools. There had been a long chat with Bomber earlier and it was just a matter of waiting for the phone call.

∞

"Where you been?" he yelled, cracking his knuckles.

"I … out."

Bevan held up his index finger, mullah style. His dry eyes glanced and glinted. Narelle just stared at him. The bruising on her face after three days had jaundiced. His bulk menaced her. She anchored further in defiance. He raised his other arm, decorated with confused ink design, fist clenched.

Bevan knew who it was. She had accidently left her phone on the kitchen table overnight. He had listened to her message bank.

She trembled but managed to keep her eyes steady. "I hate you," she said, flat, deadpan. The phone saved her.

"Ay."

It was Bomber. "It's on, man!"

∞

Bevan snorted a generous line of speed and headed to the underground railway station. The click of busy rank-and-file echoes bounced off the shiny surfaces and rumbles shivered up the ramp. He pulled his beanie down lower: it wasn't that cold. A blind hopeful played Dylan with a yawning guitar case sparsely scattered with silver coins.

He nudged the door into the men's. Bomber was standing in front of a mirror preening, and a bloke in a floral shirt was having a leak. Bevan nodded towards the end cubicle and turned away just as the other bloke squelched out.

Bomber clicked the cubicle door shut and whispered, "Got the money?"

"Yep. Got the stuff?"

Bomber pulled out a large plastic pack. "There. Let's see the money, man."

Bevan snatched the pack. "You've been doing my missus, eh old mate, haven't ya."

"Whaaaat?"

"Not only stupid but deaf too. You should be careful what you say on the bloody phone, dickhead."

Bevan's hand shot out like a moray eel, grabbed Bomber by the throat and pinned him against the cubicle wall. His other fist dealt a thudding blow to the stomach. The scrawny man had no answer for the hydraulic press around his throat. His eyes almost exploded and Bevan could feel the life of the other man slowly recede as urine and brown muck pooled on the floor.

Someone came into the toilet whistling *Alfie*.

Bevan held on, squeezing even tighter. He became aware of his hissing breath through rotten teeth. The whistling continued, the urinal flushed, a tap gushed and spat, footsteps squelched and the door opened. *Alfie* finished with the whoomp and click.

Bomber slid down the wall like a blob of custard into the reeking puddle. Bevan worked on self-control for a few seconds. He shook his head, wiped the door catch with his sleeve, and climbed over into the next cubicle where he reeled off some toilet paper. He wadded where his hands had been, then stepped quickly to the main door, nudged it, dropped the paper, and walked out.

Bevan pulled the beanie down further, popped on a pair of sunglasses, walked down the ramp to the quake of a train and fading Dylan, pockets full of product and proceeds.

∞

The cops were almost on him; the platform shook. Sweat soaked his shirt.

The tall cop said, "Let's get a coffee, Reg," and they walked straight past.

The train rumbled in; heat, air and thunder. Bevan, relieved, turned, looked at the departing leather jackets, and jumped into the carriage just as the doors swooshed closed.

The end

Where we go

Nobody knows -

Show courage when selected

GOING HOME

"Hey what're you doin' there? Who the hell are you?"
Les Moore battled his eyes into focus from sleep. He spoke to a shape in the corner. The room was very dark. "Hey! I'm talkin' to you!" Fear smouldered in the background.

"Don't be afraid, mate." The voice came from the deep. "People always fear me - they shouldn't though."

The voice had bikie menace about it, a crow from the sky. Les thought he saw the flash of teeth in a sly smile.

"Wwwell, you're in my bedroom, who *are* you?"

Les was confused and worried, with his wife there asleep alongside him.

The dark shape spoke. "Take it easy mate, I mean no harm … but I do bear bad tidings. For you."

"Bad tidings? What do you mean bad tidings."

"I'm from the Death Squad mate … don't be alarmed. You're not dead, yet." The shape chuckled and a deep-down chill went through Les like hot wire through dripping.

"Death Squad? Look, what the hell is this?" He pinched himself hard. Yes, he thought he was wide awake now.

The darkness spoke again. "My boss is Mr Emptiness … now how's that? That's his bloody name. We have a sense of humour. Anyway, he sent me. To see you."

Les squinted towards the voice. It continued.

"Mr Emptiness, he's in charge of issuing Termination Certificates."

"Termination certificates? Hey look, what the hell is this? This rubbish you're going on with?"

"You're lucky you've got me. We're darn busy at the moment; the usual person who does this is on a training course at the Cemetery Section. I'm a permanent from the Death Watch Section and I'm on temporary transfer to this job. It is just a job mate, just a job. Anyway … Les Moore?" the shape came closer, "You are on notice."

"On notice? What do you mean on notice?" Les answered, an acid skewer had penetrated his soul.

The being in the corner projected an aura of heat. A feeling of hopelessness permeated the room.

"Look, Mister Moore, everyone has to die. Andy Warthole snapped shots of himself once too often, Jack Kero-the-Wack was too out of it, on that bloody road for far too long. Buck – Charles Bukowski and that fifth of whisky, he had to go; you can't keep drinking like he did. Even your mate, yeah her, alongside you. But she's right for the moment. Everyone and everything become nothing, in the end. But you?" He raised what Les took to be a bony finger. "You will die soon."

"But I'm not ready to die," said Les, trying to ground himself even though he was confused by being woken. Now he was wide awake.

The image in black took a moment to speak. When he did there was an edge of finality in the voice. "Being ready has nothing to do with it, cobber. Nothing! Your name came up. Just like your sister's name came up that time so long ago."

Les thought for a second. Relief hovered for a second.

"I don't have a sister! Right? I don't have a bloody sister, see, you've got it wrong mister."

"Oh yes, that's right mate, but you did have a sister, forty-eight years ago."

Les' brow bunched. "Hang on, but she died at birth. They said she never made it. She didn't die. How can someone die when they don't live, eh?"

The silence in the room was like an over inflated balloon with a pin nearby.

Les' mind flashed back to that day, when he was six years old. It started to gel; his dad told him that the angels had taken away their little girl. His sister. She was dead on delivery; everyone in the family knew that.

The dark shape drew a black cloak around himself. They stared at each other.

"Oh, she was born alright mate, seven seconds. Seven bloody seconds. She lived, she died, simple arithmetic. Do the sums Mister Moore."

Les' head was full and heavy. He was about to ask how the hell this person knew. It then became apparent.

The darkness spoke again, dead-pan. "That's life mate, some people live for eighty, a hundred years, some for one second. Look, see this paperwork, here?" He held up a handful of loose sheets. "On my way here, I had to go to a place to verify the deaths of, look here, just under a hundred thousand babies born on this day, all under five seconds old."

"Vverify? Deaths, a hundred thou …"

"Yes, my old mate, umm … don't mind me calling you that do you? Well, as time after death means bugger all, time is not money. Oh yes, people on earth think it is and it may be so but not where I come from. Anyway, I had to go to the subcontinent and tick their names, if they have one, off my list. It's the paperwork you understand. Mr Emptiness, my boss, had to have them verified because he's applying for a job in the Chasm Section, umm, yeah, Decay Officer Grade Five, I think? No. That's it, OIC B and R, Bones and Rot Manager. Anyway, I may apply for his vacancy because I'm only Acting Extinction Officer Grade One. Funny thing, promotion here is sort of demotion really, down the ladder is up, if you get my direction. Anyway. *You are going to die,* my old mate, that's what you are going to do."

"Bbbut …"

The gaunt dark face appeared bonier and the depth of darkness, with a force of heat and coldness, increased. Les had never experienced the feeling, but strangely a calm softness hovered too.

"Die? When?"

There was a sniff, perhaps a smirk.

"Can't tell you, mate, even if I wanted to. I don't know. Look, I'm really a Death Watch Officer grade four, alright? But, I'm on temporary transfer and only acting in this job, you see, I'm not trusted with the exact details." The cloaked figure extended hands, not exactly pleading but ... "My brief is, mate, I'm not very skilled at this yet but I'm putting you on notice. Alright?"

Les blinked several times. It was happening alright; he touched his wife who was asleep. She mumbled and coo-ed softly. He looked towards the figure with the black cape and deep eye sockets.

"Does everybody get warned?" Les searched for words. "I mean ..."

"Yes mate, they do. Most people just get a subtle warning. But you, well you've cheated the Grand Obituary three times so far."

"How do you know that?"

There was a chuckle. "I know everything, mate, and if I don't know, well, we have the Personnel Information Sub—Section, er PISS for short. I can find anything out from them."

"Orright, when did I cheat, how ... and exactly what does cheat mean?"

"Well, Les, I can call you that can't I? Er ... it's not normal policy to be this friendly, but, well, I sort of like you, Les. Cheat? Now, remember the time when you were nearly washed off the rocks fishing? Yeah? That was one time. The other two were ... umm yes, the German measles when you were ten, and ... the car accident ... when you rolled your Holden."

Les thought for a moment, moved his eyebrows around. "Oh."

"Now, your stats fall into the three out of ten categories, and Mr Big will allow up to five. Bad luck for you but the four and five categories are for monks and holy souls. Anyway, normal humans get up to and including three brushes with the Promised Land. The computer spits out these names, and yours came up for review on The Death Squad Capital Works Program. You are on notice Mister Les Moore."

The anorexic blackness in the corner crossed and uncrossed its legs. He wrapped the black cape around his shoulders, tighter.

Les thought he was leaving so he hurriedly spoke. "Tell me when?"

"Can't mate. Don't be afraid. It comes to everyone no matter whom. You know what?"

There was no time for an answer.

"Well, like you, I was alive once." He gave a low chuckle, then a cough. "Sorry, don't mean to trivialise death old mate, but it happens as true as light and dark. Do you understand?"

"Yyyes. I think so, but please, I need to know, if you won't tell me when, then how ... please, please tell me?"

"You know what? I like you Les, you've got guts, you don't want to give up do you? Alright I shouldn't do this but, oh well, what the hell. Did you get that? What the hell? There's no such place mate, just a figment of religious people's imagination. Anyway, it says here." He unrolled a scroll. "Now, let me see, umm Hydrogen. Is that carry two? Oxygen one ... er Hydrogen Oxide ... oh yes Les, H_2O, water, that's it, water."

"Water? But what does that mean?"

"Sorry cobber, that's it. I can't tell you anymore. Look, handle it, be strong."

"Can you tell me ... er ... will it be soon?"

Les looked across the dark room. He could not see the person quite so clearly now.

"Look, Les, don't worry, it could be tomorrow. It could be two years away, because soon is anytime, even though if Mr Big spares you, say, tomorrow, well your name goes back into the R.A. system, or R.A, that's Refer Again. It used to be called Re-Submit, RS, before our office re-organisation, some called it rat sh... Anyway, then it goes on for review. Look, I must go now, I've spent too much time on you already."

The shape stood, picked up a scythe that had not been apparent before, and looked straight at Les from a face that became more skeletal and a duller incandescence. The eyes intensified momentarily and glowed like brake lights. Then he dissolved into the heavy air.

Les Moore rubbed his eyes and continued to look but the room became darker. He touched his wife. She slept soundly. He looked harder again into the corner but no one was there.

∞

Les woke up with a jump. He felt like he had not slept. What had happened? It seemed all so real. Could it have been a dream? He felt for his wife but she was not there. He sat bolt upright.

"Hey Les, why don't ya get up, ya lazy blighter? Brekkie's ready, hun," warbled his wife from the kitchen.

He sank back in the bed for a moment or two, relieved. Many things went through his head as he shuffled out to the table.

"Struth, Les, you look like ya didn't sleep a wink last night. You alright, bub? The full moon Les, that's what did it. The full moon always affects you like that."

"Umm, yeah I s'pose."

"Ya shouldn't a had that great big joint before ya hit the cot; ya know that stuff always gets your brain ticking over."

"Yeah."

"I tell ya what Les, Cuthbert barked all bloody night too. Full moon, does it every time. Hey hun? Why does Blerta give his dogs such silly names?" She shook her head at the silliness of blokes.

"What? Yeah."

Les managed a smile at his lovely wife as she walked out of the kitchen. Not a bad looking woman, he thought, even if she was getting on a bit in years. Just then his eyes became bulbous. *It was a bright night last night, full moon. Aaaaaah! Must have been a dream. That bloke in the corner was in the dark, hard to see.*

"Must have been a dream."

"What was that hun?" His wife stuck her head around the door.

"Er, she's right, just singin'," replied Les. He felt better now. *Phew! Just a dream.*

∞

For the next couple of months Les was reasonably measured in his life activities. Not that he feared dying, of course. Nah. If he was, he wouldn't have admitted it to anyone. However, the experience of that night had an impact on him. Even though he was almost certain it was a dream, he took a few steps to change his routine. He found himself thinking more about daily activities and if there were any dangers or not. Les gave up smoking cigarettes and drinking beer; for a while, anyway. Much to his wife's surprise he stopped smoking dope, which she, and indeed he, would have thought impossible.

One day as she was pouring a glass of wine, she turned to him. "Are you alright, Les?"

He nodded and smiled.

She continued. "You haven't found God, have you?"

He smiled. "Nah ... just decided to ease up a bit on some things, that's all."

She was not convinced, but being a veteran of relationships, she knew men did all sorts of things for all sorts of reasons. Les was no exception. She lifted her eyebrows, took a sip, and went out into the garden.

For almost three months Les stayed away from water in general, except for his daily shower. No swimming; that was not anything out of the ordinary as he did not swim much, and there were no fishing trips. He was not a keen angler anyway so that did not matter. The experience of that night slowly faded and Les Moore carried on with his life, working and living.

One day on his way to the city he rounded a bend. A truck was stopped in the middle of the road. In that fraction of a second his heart leapt as he wrenched the wheel with instant strength but slippery fingers.

"Rooooooooooooooooooooooooooooooooooot!" he screamed as the lack of weight in the back of the vehicle caused the ute to pirouette out of control and then it smashed through the safety barrier. The cold dark swirling river swallowed the car in moments.

∞

The police officer touched him gently on the side of the neck as the winch secured the dripping vehicle on to the bank.

Les squinted. "Hey mate ... er ... officer, get an ambulance quick, I'm hurt pretty bloody bad. See? Look at this, my arm, and my head? I've got a sore head! Surely you can see I need assistance?"

The Officer shook his head sadly and seemed to look straight through him for a second or two. Then he stood up and yelled above the thundering water and the noise of the diesel tow truck up on the bank. "Hey Cable, we got ourselves a carcass here, mate."

Les screamed, "Carcass? Hey … I'm still alive. Can't ya see? I need help!"

Just then Les noticed a dark shape behind the police officer. He knew who it was straight away.

"He can't hear you, Les."

Les ran a quivering wet hand over his bleeding face and shook his head. "What do you mean, can't hear me?"

"Exactly that mate." The dark shape in the black cloak spoke with authority. "You are dead, mate. *Dead set dead.* Don't be afraid. I'm here to guide you. I've got the forms here, see?"

He rested the scythe against his shoulder and held up a document. Les was close enough to see that it was a photograph of himself as a child.

Just then the Police Officer yelled, "Hey Cable, hang on! I think this bloke's still alive; I reckon his lips moved, quick help me drag him out."

Les looked at the shape in the cloak and even though in pain he managed a small smile. He tried to give the finger as if to say, "See mate I'm not dead."

The tow truck operator and the policeman hurriedly dragged him out of the wreck. The cop continued to give him CPR.

Les looked straight up at the shape in the black cloak who was now standing above them and yelled with genuine relief, "Look, I'm not dead, I'm not dead!"

The darkness looked on with eyes like a currawong.

The policeman stopped CPR. "Aaaah hell, naaah! We've lost him, he's had the raspberry," and he turned to Steve Cable. "I could have sworn his lips moved though; it was worth a try anyway."

"Hey officer," screamed Les, "I'm not dead. *I'm not dead!*"

"Bloody hell Cable, seein' someone cark it … ya never get used to it, mate I tell ya, never. He seemed like he came back to us for a sec, then …"

"Les? Look at me mate? It's me, Acting Extinction Officer Grade One. They can't hear you. I have no choice but to pronounce you dead." The Grim Reaper held up a form and placed a big red X in the box at the bottom. "All we have to do now, mate, is file this. Forms, eh? Office procedure. Simple. I'm taking you home Les Moore. It's where we all go in the end. There's nothing beyond."

The end

Be gracious

Take timely advice

Being wrong is not a sin

GYPSY KINGS

"Let's take the train," yelled Nellie.

"What?" Ralph tried to communicate above the din of the remonstrating taxi drivers. The traffic noise, punctuated by the biting bark of motorbikes in the mid-30s heat, did not help.

Being told it was easy to get a taxi from Naples to Sorrento was an oxymoron. The moron who advised them was a know-all who had done it ten or more years ago.

Nellie grabbed the handle of her new *you-beaut, multi-directional everyone's got to have one* suitcase, and took off back towards the doors of the railway station. Ralph was left to explain to the poor taxi official - at least he wore a high-vis jacket to identify him so - that they had decided to go by train and they no longer needed a taxi.

The other dozen or so taxi drivers and touts pushed and shoved each other and tried to tell Ralph that each of the others was with the Mafia. He could not help thinking that they were all Mafia. They seemed to complicate the situation by each further claiming that Ralph and Nellie had promised to go with each of them individually, which of course was not true.

There was frantic arm waving, chests exposing gold or silver crosses getting tangled up with buttons and chest hair and a noise level he had not experienced for many years. With the possibility of them being Mafia, he thought the knives might come out soon, so he quickly ducked under a barrier and divorced himself from the throng, but he did not escape the threatening barrage of language that came from their direction. He understood a little Italian but no swear or abusive words. He could not decipher any of the language that followed him.

Ralph joined Nellie just inside the sliding doors, patting his pockets to reassure himself that everything was there. He managed a small smile, remembering the argument he had with Nellie when he purchased his cargo shorts. At least the noise level inside was more subdued.

"Thanks for leaving me with the Mafia," he said.

Nellie changed the subject; she was good at that. "Go over and ask at the tourist information counter." She was good at giving orders, too. "Ah, closed as expected." The last bit was said with a slight acid edge.

In July, mid-summer, at the Naples railway station in overloaded air-conditioning they were amongst people from everywhere, tourists and locals alike. Ralph was not that keen on travelling in Europe in peak season during the hottest summer on record. He was also a bit unenthusiastic because Nellie seemed hell-bent on spending their entire superannuation in one trip.

So far, they had done the hard slog since flying into Marco Polo airport; travelling by bus *and* train and organising it themselves as they went. Over a beer with mates at a future time, he might be amused by the fact that *only* the officials in these conglomerates seemed to know where to buy tickets and of course, what bay or platform the mode of transport departed from. But right now, it was frustrating.

His thoughts wandered back several hours when they had to purchase their tickets from Florence to Naples. Nellie of course, always gave him a task if it was difficult, so she could have a go at him, if, and or when, it went wrong. He was after all in charge of buying the tickets and by the time he found the correct counter, he felt as if he had physically aged several years. After being bustled and shoved and having people push in front of him, he finally got the tickets. But the fun was not over, because they still had to find the platform. They stood gazing stupidly at the electronic noticeboard along with hundreds of other people just as bewildered as they were.

At least Nellie contributed by pointing, "That's our train there, Ralph." It was not much help as far was he was concerned, but it was better than nothing. Having the train identified was not the whole picture either because the platform number was not indicated. They had twenty minutes to spare, but he was still edgy, his forehead felt warm.

No platform number had appeared with ten minutes to go. Through what Nellie insisted was clever deduction, she declared that their train had to be leaving from either platform two or platform three.

She frowned. "Ralph, go and ..."

Ralph was not sure on her deductions, but he was not going to argue either, so he took off. He was not surprised to find those platforms did not appear to exist, but further investigation located them to the side of the main area. They were not clearly marked and only visible if you stumbled through a series of arches. During this time his ears were hammered with ear-splitting, indecipherable announcements that bounced and echoed and competed with the train noises and the massive crowd. He rushed back to join Nellie and the others who stared up at the electronic noticeboard as if Superman was up in the sky.

"I think I've found them," he said, glancing up at the train number and the still not yet identified platform number. "Bloody hell," he continued, "four minutes to go."

Ralph's heart hammered and blobs of sweat trickled down his spine. It was obvious that other travellers were experiencing similar problems, because if it was possible, the noise level increased, and people became more agitated. Then, as if someone in the office had experienced a brainwave, the number of the platform flashed up with two minutes to go.

It was platform number nine, not two or three, but they did not have time to concern themselves with that detail. He was not game to point it out to her either because Nellie was not very good at admitting being wrong. They rushed towards platform nine, along with what seemed like hundreds of other people, just as the super bullet train pulled in.

It seemed to Ralph like opening day at the Royal Show or Boxing Day sales. They stood behind the line, thinking they were doing the right thing but they were almost on their own because their fellow passengers were trying to get on the train as the alighting passengers were trying to get off. He did not think there was any need to worry too much because they had numbered seats and if you had numbered seats, surely no one else could sit in them, could they?

As rare fortune would have it, he was right, or nearly right, because there were several backpackers sitting in their seats and they were not keen to move, until Ralph produced his tickets and pulled rank with his age. The seat allocation involved sections with alphabetical identification as well as numbers and was ambiguous at best. Most of the other people seemed to be confused about that, so they were not the only ones.

Ralph relaxed once they got going and he occupied his mind watching the monitor, checking his watch, and looking out the window at vehicles on the road. The monitor showed the train reached a top speed of 299 kilometres per hour. Nellie was reasonably good at being relaxed if she could find someone to do the worrying for her. The trip from Florence to Naples took only a few hours and it was a clean train with waiter service.

∞

Back in Naples.

Fortunately, the train from Naples to Sorrento was relatively easy to locate as the platform number was on the ticket but it seemed to Ralph as if everyone in the world was going to Sorrento. The carriages appeared more like a tram car than proper train carriages. All were grubby and covered in graffiti, but the budding artists had at least spared patches of window area, so passengers could look out. They let two crowded trains lumber by, chockers with people, ten minutes apart before they decided that all the trains would be crowded, and they would be waiting some time before there was one that was not.

It was a major task to struggle with their bags through the whooshing doors into the already crowded compartment. Now that they were on their way to Sorrento, Ralph was able to relax a little even though they were crammed in, shoulder to shoulder with passengers.

The seats were divided almost equally between tourists and locals and it was difficult, if not impossible, to move down the aisles because of suitcases, boxes, bags, and those standing. People seemed to accept the fact that it was crowded, and everyone had to share whatever meagre space was available. It was extremely hot as the air-conditioning system consisted of windows that could be opened and windows that were broken. The locals, seemingly going to or from work just nodded and smiled. This was obviously normal to them. The door pressed the last one in and the train rattled along on the milk run in the direction of Sorrento. The first few stations only added more passengers and Ralph and Nellie were crammed even further into the standing up area opposite the opening doors.

Whilst battling the leaning, lurching, and jerking, Ralph was nudged to one side and squashed even further up against someone standing beside him.

The bloke smiled. "Orr wight then?" Obvious cockney greeting.

Ralph replied, "Sorry, mate, bit crowded."

"You can say that again. First time away?"

Ralph did not want to tell lies but stretching the truth was alright. "Nup. Did a cruise last year and been to a few places, er overseas." He did not want to admit that those few places were Tasmania, New Zealand, and Kangaroo Island.

"We come to Italy every year," said the man, nodding towards his wife. "Love the sun and the beaches, know wot I mean?"

The train clickety-clacked past old buildings smothered in graffiti and any usable ground had grid patterns of tomato plants and olive trees. Ralph smiled in acknowledgement but wondered why he and Nellie came *from* the sun *to* the sun with their Celtic skin. His body was punctuated with the evidence of sunspot removals.

The bloke winked, "Watch your pockets, know wot I mean? Up around Rome is all wight, but down here, near Naples, well the people are a bit poorer like …"

The train jerked and lurched and everyone hung on as it accelerated and then just as quickly slowed down to round the corner.

"No worries, there," replied Ralph, patting the pockets of his cargo shorts. "Had quite an argument with the missus before we left home about money belts and things."

The train pulled into a station, a couple of people got off and three musicians and one passenger crammed in. Immediately loud music erupted as the train pulled away - drums, squeeze box and a small guitar. It was what was needed to take everyone's minds off the hot, cramped conditions. People smiled and swayed with the train and loud gypsy, zydeco music. Some of the tourists took photographs, the locals just smiled and looked out the grubby, cracked windows as the train continued, losing, and gaining passengers on the way. They passed obviously obsolete stations, covered with weeds and debris, with piles of sleepers and old railway carriages no longer in use. It was clear everyone loved the music because as one of their number climbed up and down the aisle, most people threw money in the tin. Ralph and the man next to him threw some Euros in as well.

The music continued with great gusto and ceased just as quickly as the moving human lump of carriage pulled into the next station. The musicians, Gypsy Kings yelled, *Grazie*! and stepped off with others and suddenly there was more room. Two more stations and the announcement barked in a battle-axe voice that Sorrento was next.

Ralph noticed the bloke next to him patting his pockets. Trying not to look rattled, Ralph gently slid his hand down to the pocket in his cargo shorts. He looked up; Nellie was looking directly at him, eyes wide. She was spot on. Ralph glanced down at his naked wrist. Watch? Gone. Wallet? Gone. He glanced quickly around, others feeling their pockets with horrified faces.

The end

Everything has purpose

Hard to see - for some

Is there a toll in the end?

THE BELL

"What's the stupid thing for, can't see no church around here."
Kevin *Leech* Doolan, wiped his nose on a dirty, denim sleeve.

"It's to warn people in case of fire," replied Hans *Gecko* Kresser, pensively stroking his bum-fluff beard.

Leech was new to the area. He threw a bottle at the bell and missed. Not satisfied, he heaved a rock and hit it.

Bong!

"Let's pull the bastard down, eh?" suggested Leech, hawking on the ground nearby.

"Hell, that's gunna require more effort than I'm prepared to give it," puffed Gecko. The walk around the site had worn him out. "Anyway, why?" He asked, scratching his head.

"Come on," persisted Leech, ignoring him, as he grabbed a length a steel cable from the back of the ute.

"Hey Leech? Umm ... why?"

"Who gives a root; they don't need no bell!" He generally struggled to express himself clearly. The idea of doing something anti-social always appealed to Leech.

"But it's there for a reason, I think." His gecko eyes looked bigger than usual. He scratched his head and frowned at his mate.

"Come on, you gunna lend a hand or not?" Leech had already chucked a snigging chain over the beam that held the bell.

"Fair enough, I suppose, someone has to drive." Gecko somehow felt obliged to be part of it.

"Just as well, it's your ute," laughed Leech, spitting again.

Gecko dumped his pudgy frame into the driver's seat, closed the door and hit the starter. Meanwhile, Leech, hooked up both ends of the cable.

"Right, take the strain."

Gecko rested his chin on his bicep as he looked in the exterior rear vision mirror, the arm sported a new tattoo, an eagle with roses around the edge. He might have been concentrating too much on how good his slicked back black hair looked, because his foot slipped off the clutch. The car lurched forward, almost ripping out the back end of the ute.

"You bloody dope," whooped Leech, almost falling over laughing. "Just as well it's your car".

"Righto, yeah alright, shut up, will ya?"

The next time he took it easy, gradually taking the strain and the vehicle easily pulled over the huge gantry. The bell hit the ground with a complex thudding boonk.

Leech let out a long whoop. "That'll fix them bastards. Righto, let's chuck it over the waterfall."

"Er … what, but why?"

"Because we can, stupid head. Anyway, it'll make a nice big *ding* when she hits the bottom, right?"

Leech rolled his sleeves up over bony elbows, undid the snigging chain, and then spat on his hands. "Come on, you lazy prick, let's go." He started grunting. The job was underway as far as he was concerned.

"But listen here, Leech, why are we doing this?"

"Look, shut your trap and come and give us a hand, will ya?"

Gecko's brow darkened again. "Hell, it's pretty bloody heavy, mate."

"I told you, shut ya head!"

With superhuman effort, they dragged the two and a half hundredweight bell to the top of the waterfall. Sweat mingled with the puffing and panting.

Leech pulled out a packet of rollies, "I need a smoke."

He put out a stream of tobacco into a cigarette paper, rolled and lit it, then threw the makings to Gecko. They sat back, two young blokes, smoking and watching the approaching glassy water babble over rocks smoothed by hundreds of years. Then the water quickened and gathered in a smaller spout, preparing for the thunderous drop of ten metres to the frothing pool at the bottom. Leech stood up, stretched, and taking one last drag, flicked the butt into the bush.

"Hey, you could start a fire doing that." Gecko went over and ground out the cigarette butt. He turned to remonstrate but was not quick enough.

"That wouldn't start no fire, you dick-head, bush ain't dry enough," said Leech strongly, squatting down. "Right, let's get this bell movin', old mate."

They pushed, heaved, and dragged the huge lump of brass over the boulders towards the edge of the waterfall. Jeans wet to the knees, worn low enough, both sported wedgies. Socks became blotters for their boots. At last, they had the bell teetering right on the edge.

"I wanna be part of this," gushed Gecko quickly, somehow thinking he might miss out on the grand finale.

They both pushed the bell one last time, grunting bodies and gripping feet. It rolled awkwardly for a few inches on the sharp decline making muffled anvil noises, raging water nudged and rolled it with gathering momentum. Hidden power mauled and muscled it closer to the edge. The deep-down grunt of the torrent played with it for a moment and then pushed it over. Although the waterfall continued to roar, seconds froze.

Time clicked in again and there was an enormous splash, followed immediately by a thumping, muffled depth charge.

"Hell, that was a bit piss-poor," expressed Leech, goozying over the waterfall. "I thought we'd get a better ding than that."

"Yeah, er ... why did we do that? Hey mate, let's, umm piss off out of here."

"You've got no guts, Gecko. Who gives a root about no fire and who cares about a stupid bell?"

∞

"Bloody hell," yelled Assistant Fire Officer Sam *Sparks* Harvey, eyeing the approaching thundering bushfire.

Acting Senior Fire Warden Eddie Coles re-adjusted his helmet. "Gee mate, we're gunna have to get the hell out of here. She's heading this way and also spreading out into the valley." He jumped into the driver's seat and continued, "Pity about the bell, some bastard pinched it. We can't warn anyone. Anyway mate, who lives out that way?"

The whoosh and roar combined with the fierce crackle and rifle pop of the swirling fire made it hard to talk. They could feel the radiant heat at the truck.

Sparks dived in the passenger side. "Only two houses, I think, according to this." He consulted a clipboard. "Two families, let me see, yeah the Kressers and the Doolans."

"Come on mate, let's go!" Eddie hit the key, and the motor burst into life.

"But Eddie, we just can't leave ..." Sparks remonstrated with his spare hand.

"Listen mate," he yelled, winding up the window, "The speed that fire's approaching, we're rooted if we don't go right bloody-well now!"

The end

Respect differences

When all in together -

And enjoy the trip

BROKEN

Yesterday had taken its toll - organising money, accommodation, and tickets, in blistering, drenching tropical heat. This morning had not won any prizes either, but finally Trevor and Ruth stumbled into the departure area of the Flores airport in Indonesia. They should have felt relaxed but tense sweat soaked their clothes, just as bad as it had outside.

Ruth frowned and pointed at the sign, *Broken,* taped under the fan switches. "I've seen that word before."

The fan and light in their room had been broken. The aggressive mosquitoes ignored the coils and the boiling humid heat robbed them of anything that resembled sleep. The fridge in the restaurant had been broken and the taxi to the airport had been broken. Fortunately, the taxi became unbroken quickly when they shelled out wads of rupiah.

Passengers' attention was jolted back to reality in the airport lounge. Some official had fixed the connection on the speaker system and decided to turn the volume up. The *Bee Gees Greatest Hits* came on and although loud, was a genuinely welcomed break from the intermittent previous static of *Kenny G.* The two flickering monitors showed different departure times. Obviously, the plane was late.

Trevor and Ruth quietly discussed the *electric problem.* A German lady told them a few minutes ago that there was a slight *electric problem* with the plane from East Timor. Something had been broken but was now fixed. The plane in question was the supposed jet aircraft with propellers, they were about to catch.

Yesterday, the airline official, with a fine array of piano keys for teeth, told them their mode of transport was a jet. Trevor had pointed to a poster covered in black fly dots showing a propeller aircraft. The man informed them that it was a jet aircraft with propellers. At the time they smiled at each other, just happy to be able to get off the island.

It was pointless reading their novels because the *Bee Gees Greatest Hits* hammered out at such a high-volume.

Just then excited talk increased and the German lady nearby commented, "I think de plane iss coming. See, maybe de electric problem iss fixed." She added with an element of alarm, "Oooh! The fire brigadier iss going. Look!"

Fifty or more faces, whether they understood English or not, peered out the window to see the *jet aircraft* with propellers from East Timor touch down. The *fire brigadier* consisted of a rusty, red early model Kejang Ute with a group of young men hanging on to the sides as it sped out to the approaching aircraft. They had trouble hanging on to the water containers and red buckets of sand. Trevor and Ruth exchanged glances.

The ute returned without any apparent incident because the lads were laughing and throwing water over each other. The *jet aircraft* with propellers taxied up to the terminal. The din increased.

Before the propellers were cut, the airline official felt it necessary to open the double doors. The noise accelerated beyond belief and the terminal filled with fumes, dust, and flying scraps of debris. Some keen passengers allowed their excitement to get the better of them and they headed for the stairs which were not even in position. With the help of several other staff the eager ones were herded back inside. The Australians had come to terms with the fact that the arrival of any mode of transport in Asia always created a high level of excitement. The doors were then closed again and the terminal suffered stifling heat, with the addition of the dust and fumes. Then the passengers coming from the east filed in.

Every man, woman and child in the terminal scrutinised the faces of the new arrivals for fear, or other signs of a perilous journey. Trevor and Ruth were very good at being near the head of the line in case boarding took place. As the *Bee Gees* hammered out for the third time *The World is Round*, they watched the luggage go out to the aircraft, both thinking it could be the last they would see of them.

DING DONG DING! A deafening, distorted chime almost blew the speakers off the wall. The only advantage was that the *Bee Gees* song was temporarily halted. A female voice chattered something. Most people seemed to understand, but they were Indonesians. Trevor would not have understood it, even if it was in English, because his hearing was not very good and the announcement was badly distorted.

A stampede, like wildebeest, swarmed towards the double doors. Trevor and Ruth were ready, their experience told them that any announcement meant, *Grab ya gear and go like mad*. The Australians were able to force their way near the frontrunners.

The airline official screamed, "Transit passajjer only!" forcing a gossamer of spit on those nearby. No one took any notice and he was physically picked up and carried backwards. The double glass doors fortunately opened with the impact and he ended up in a heap, trampled. His uniform looked as if it had come out of a cement mixer. No one seemed to care as they battled towards the aircraft some twenty metres away. People power walked to the stairs and pushed and shoved each other trying to be first.

Ruth felt strongly about women's rights, particularly Muslim women who usually had to walk behind their husbands, but she was shocked at the sight before her. The women pushed everyone out of the way, including their husbands. Such was the frenzy to get on that plane. Fighting for a seat on any mode of transport in Asia seemed to have that effect on people.

Trevor used his tired six-foot frame to hold position and apart from kneeing a nun up the backside, accidentally, he was the fifth one onboard. He managed to hold two seats right over the wing with a staggered view as the seats were not coordinated with the windows.

They considered themselves very lucky as it was blatantly obvious there were more tickets sold than seats available.

Ruth grabbed Trevor's hand. Her blue eyes stared and she whispered, "Let's not get too cocky about our situation, eh?"

She attempted to fasten her seat belt and realized with a degree of alarm that it was broken. Instead of looking at Trevor she tried to breathe deeply while glancing out of the grubby cracked Perspex window. The string of *Brokens* was bad enough, but she had great difficulty suppressing the *Electric Problem* from her mind.

The end

Be wary

Where trust is concerned

In faraway places

PRICE OF LIBERTY

Today.

The knock was sharp. Charlie shook sleep from his head. He opened the door. A big, muscled, uniformed officer burst in and pushed him backwards. He hit the wall and landed awkwardly on the bed. A senior police officer with a polished walnut complexion and black handlebar moustache pointed a short piece of cane.

"Passport!" The command was as sharp as the knock on the door.

∞

Two days earlier.

"Hey buddy, interested?" The young bloke with blond hair and floral shirt leaned across from a table of four and held out a joint. "Hash."

Charlie did not think, he did not need to. "Yeah, thanks."

Vasco's Restaurant provided a spot to take in the last few moments of the hot, humid day. The bamboo tables were strategically placed just above high tide on the sand. Open air with palm-frond roof, casual and comfortable.

"Thanks, mate." Charlie handed it back, blowing a geyser of smoke up towards the fan.

Small talk resumed at the other table. He leant back in a dream-state and looked at the gentle waves tumbling towards the last of

the strolling humans on the beach. The high humidity and the 30°
temperature of Goa were not much different to Brisbane.

"You never actually see the sun drop below the horizon, man,"
offered the American, angling his head. "My name is Grover, by the
way, how ya doin'?"

"Charlie."

They shook hands.

"Mind if I take a seat?" His speech dragged. It was obvious to
Charlie he'd had more than one smoke.

"No worries. Umm, why don't you see the sun drop below the
horizon?"

"Well," smiled Grover, dropping his short frame into the cane
chair, "in the tropics when the sun gets low in the sky, like now, for
some strange reason, man, a row of clouds seems to be lying just
above the horizon, they just appear from nowhere - see?"

Charlie Carter, comfortably whacked, looked out towards the
horizon where the orange sun boiled. He could not really see the row
of clouds.

Grover continued. "You watch, man. We may need a couple beers
here, within the next one-half hours."

Charlie looked at his empty Kingfisher tallie. At a couple of
dollars each it was a hell of a lot cheaper than home.

Grover leaned and waved towards the bar. "Hey Rod, couple
Kingfishers here, thanks, man." He turned to Charlie. "Rodriguez, cool
dude, no worries, you know, blowing J's in here, man, they don't mind."

Kingfishers arrived. Glass clinked.

"See man, look? The sun is going out of sight, true to the legend."

They looked out towards the horizon as the now blood red sun
smoothly eased behind the strip of clouds not there before. A scatter
of traditional fishing boats drifted at distances from the shore. The
earlier slight breeze had dropped, and the sea was a metal sheen in
the damping light. The small waves continued to gently whoosh on
to a steep shore guarded by coconut palm sentries.

"Amazing, bloody amazing," said Charlie.

Grover pulled out a pre-rolled joint and lit up. The pleasant acrid
smell of hash and fresh tobacco filled the air. "When did you arrive, man?"

Charlie had the feeling he was going to enjoy himself in Goa. "Four days ago, direct flight from Brisbane, short stopover in Singas."

"Aussie, eh?" He took a big tug on the joint and handed it to Charlie. "Couldn't ya tell?"

"Well, man, I thought you were, but you could have been from Noo Zeeland. How long you here for?"

Charlie smiled. "About a month, mate. How long have you been here?"

"Too long, man, too long. Say, man, interested in any hash or pills? I don't bother with grass 'cos the hash is so good."

"Maybe."

Charlie's mates who came last year blew hash joints the whole time. They said the authorities did not really care so long as you did not deal it. Ecstasy tablets were available everywhere too; if you did not have trafficable amounts, the cops apparently did not care. His mates said they met someone who had been caught with hash and a couple of pills and he was told not to do it again. After all, Goa was the party capital of the world.

"I don't think I'll worry about pills, maybe some other time." Charlie was not too keen on taking any E's because there was no way of knowing the content.

"No problem, man. Everyone's doing it."

The joint went between them.

"Anyway, yeah, I might just be interested in a small amount of hash."

"Five hundred roops a block."

"Same stuff we're smoking?" Grover nodded. "How big is a block?"

"Oh, about half as big as a matchbox."

Charlie looked out at the glassy sea. Five hundred rupees represented about ten bucks. Half as big as a match box? Things were safe and cool.

"Yeah, no worries, mate, I'm interested. Got it on you?"

"Naaah, don't like to carry any quantity with me, man, you know how it is? Even though it's cool, still need to be careful. Will have it for you tomorrow, buddy."

"Okay, mate, I'm in. What time?"

"How about midday? Where ya staying, dude?" Grover ground out the butt in a seashell ashtray in the middle of a genuine driftwood table. Ants scurried.

"The Steep Beach. Know it?"

"That's down the end, isn't it?"

"Yeah, I think so, still getting my bearings."

"How about we meet at Sazoras, it's just on the left, first bar-restaurant you hit from the main street. Okay? Can't miss it. Round noon?"

Charlie smiled. "No worries, see you there."

Grover stood, pulled out some rupees.

"I'll get it, mate," said Charlie. "My shout."

"Shout?"

"Yeah, means my round, umm, treat?"

"You Down-Unders, you dudes are a riot," laughed Grover. "Thanks buddy, see you tomorrow." He waved towards the bar, "Thanks guys," then mumbled something to the other table of three and walked out into the evening. The sun had disappeared, low level light hovered.

Charlie stretched his long legs and lit up a duty-free Marlboro as the tropical darkness descended. He did not want to wait until full darkness because of the dogs. It was not wise to wander alone at night because of the packs of street dogs. He already had a healthy respect for the dogs of Goa because of the canines near the hotel. He smiled, recalling what a South African bloke said to him coming home from one of the clubs a couple of nights ago. 'They bleff easy, but ef they bleddy surr-round you, you kuck the nearest bleddy mongrel as horde ez you ken. If you only hev sendells, then check a big bleddy steck et the bestard'.

It was light enough to feel safe and just dark enough to see the lights of Candolim. Charlie was getting to know his way around town already.

∞

Today.

Charlie, barely decent in jocks, tried to push through last night's drink and fuzz.

"I will not be requesting this again!"

The row of white teeth under the moustache was not part of a smile. Pressed khaki uniform and the colours on the epaulettes indicated rank. He stepped into the room and shoved the door closed with an elbow.

Charlie grabbed his bum-bag. The big junior officer flinched like a waiting cat. "It's in here." The officer relaxed and moved to the side as Charlie fumbled out his passport.

"My name is Inspector Rosario Fernandez of the Panaji Drug Arm." He snatched the document and turned the pages.

"What … what is this?" stammered Charlie. "Is there a problem?"

No one answered. The big junior officer continued to rummage through his rucksack. He stopped and held up a bag of marijuana.

"Yes, Mr Carter. There most certainly is a problem." Inspector Fernandez tapped his cane lightly against the edge of the passport. The silver badge on his peak cap glinted in a harsh strip of morning light through the shutter.

Charlie remained still. Sweat trickled down his spine. "What? That … that isn't mine." He hoped they did not look in his sneakers where the hash was hidden.

"Ah, Mr Carter, you have been a foolish traveller, haven't you?"

The fan, on low speed, clicked and wobbled. It made no difference to the sweat on Charlie's face.

∞

Two days earlier.

The night after the meeting with Grover, Charlie hung around the Steep Beach Hotel. He sat at the bar mostly on his own, thinking. He knew when he returned to Australia some serious decisions had to be made. Laura was pushing towards marriage. He was not ready, just twenty-six years old, too young. Did he love her? She was not happy about him going to Goa, especially without her. Charlie went to bed, his mind full but determined to enjoy himself over the next couple of weeks.

∞

Today.

The bulky junior officer continued his search. It did not take long.

"Sir? Sir?" He held up the small block of hash.

Inspector Fernandez nodded, "I think you had better come along with us, Mr Carter. You are under arrest."

Charlie shook his pounding head; blobs of sweat sprayed his knees. "Hang on, you can't just ..."

"I think it most pertinent that you are being quiet, Mr Carter."

The junior officer grabbed the bum-bag and stuffed the marijuana and hash in a bigger cloth bag.

"Now, get dressed." The inspector slid the passport into his top pocket, whipped the cane under his arm and spun on a precise heel.

Charlie fumbled his way into some clothing. The junior officer wrenched his hands in front and clicked cuffs in a practiced move. An iron grip hoisted him up and shoved him hard. Inspector Fernandez opened the door and led the way out past the boy on the front desk who avoided Charlie's eyes. A uniformed driver opened the back door of a waiting police four-wheel-drive with a purple light on top. Charlie was muscled in and the junior officer piled in alongside. The inspector barked something, and they sped out the gates, past the lounging security guards of the Steep Beach Hotel.

The heat of the sun tried to wear a hole in the roof. The breeze through the windows was a welcome relief. Rice fields, palms and patches of jungle gave way to small villages. Charlie's hands shook. Closing his eyes changed nothing.

∞

Yesterday.

On previous mornings Charlie ate the hotel breakfast. The bread was stale and sweet, and the coffee was terrible. He thought it a pity because the restaurant served great food for other meals. He decided to wander to the main road and have a marsala dosa. There were a couple of places where he was told Westerners could get reasonable coffee as well.

The Steep Beach Hotel was built in the Portuguese, terracotta-tiled, villa style using local red stone, some rendered. It was located about a kilometre from the main drag along a narrow strip of bruised bitumen that ran parallel to the beach. Several other similar types of buildings commanded wonderful views of the ocean. Some of these magnificent buildings were almost derelict and just used to store fishing nets. Inland, rice fields chequered the landscape with mathematical precision and the occasional water buffalo wallowed or ploughed under the watchful eye of a boy with stick. Small tufts of thick growth and groups of coconut palms shielded small thatched farmhouses from the concentrated tropical sun.

A couple of motorbikes played last minute chicken with Charlie as he wandered along the bitumen. Three local girls, with baskets of washing on their heads, covered their faces and giggled greetings. He looked back at their lithe bodies in translucent saris. Two local dogs followed him for a while before losing interest.

He picked a table near the fan at Xavier's and ordered an American breakfast. The waiter arrived with the coffee and dropped a copy of The Times of India on the table. The next hour or so drifted pleasantly as did the passing parade along the main road. Ancient hippies, middle-aged battlers, couples, groups of men and women, young and old, from everywhere on earth, mixed with locals, all battling the tooting traffic on the melting strip of rough bitumen. Nearing mid-day, he changed money and headed to the main beach of Candolim. On the way be bought some cigarette papers from a boy squatting with his produce in the shade of a blue poly-tarp.

Charlie stepped under the thatched awning of Sazoras out of the heat. Grover was not there so he slumped at an isolated table and grabbed a menu. It was just afternoon by the clock on the wall over the bar, so he ordered a tall beer and glanced out at the magnificent old traditional wooden fishing boats above the high-water mark. Just as he took the first sip, he felt a tap on the shoulder.

"How ya doin', buddy?" Grover pulled up a cane chair.

"Not bad thanks, mate."

"Looks like you're starting early, eh dude?"

Charlie laughed. "Can I get you one?"

"No thanks, man. I'm on a bit of a time constriction thing."

Someone out the back put on Ry Cooder, Crossroads.

∞

Today.

They rattled and swerved in the Panaji traffic. The handcuffs were tight, Charlie's hands hurt. He shook his head.

"Sir?" Leaning forward hurt. "Sir, what is … where are you taking me?"

Inspector Fernandez did not react. The junior officer elbowed him in the chest hard and wagged an index finger.

Charlie was left to his own thoughts. He closed his eyes wondering why he had been so bloody stupid as to get into this situation. Possibilities trickled into his head. Australian Embassy? Lawyer?

The car swayed as they came off the bitumen and slowed down through the gates of the police station. The driver babbled something to an officer leaning on the gate as the mighty concrete pillars and stone stairs of colonial Portuguese architecture loomed up. They chugged past the entrance and pulled up in a cloud of dust around to the side of the building.

The junior officer jumped out. "You! Here!"

Charlie's shirt was wet again, sweat beaded his forehead. A dog looked at him.

∞

Yesterday.

Grover removed his sunglasses. "Still want some hash, man?"

"Yep. Can I have a look?"

"Sure, man. Got the loot?"

"How much?"

"Five hundred Roops." Grover casually looked towards the bar and the kitchen area. He pulled a small plastic packet out of his pocket and kept it below table level. "Good shit, man."

Someone turned the music up. A puppy came over to their table, wagging its tail. A staff member clapped his hands and the dog shot off. Charlie slipped five hundred rupees inside the menu, Grover grabbed the money, and slid the menu back with the hash inside.

Grover put his sunglasses back on. "Okay dude, got to run, maybe catch you at Vasgos some time. Hope you enjoy the puff."

They shook hands and the American wandered off towards the main road.

∞

Today.

Charlie followed Inspector Fernandez up a concrete ramp past a group of people squatting and talking loudly. They did not pay any attention to him. An officer at a small desk with a pedestal fan blowing hot air, waved them through a battered wooden door into a long, dirty, bruised-ochre walled corridor. Charlie knew he needed to rise above the fear hammering inside. Because he was on the move, he told himself not to shake anymore. He could feel the hot curry breath of the junior officer behind as he followed the square shoulders and precise clicking heels of the Inspector. They passed several uniformed policemen and a collection of doors, some open. Voices of authority bounced around the shiny surfaces. A loud, desperate cry streaked from one of the rooms. The dull thudding scuffle followed, and his tremor kicked off again.

They arrived at a grubby, hand-soiled, cream-coloured door marked *PDA Questioning Room*. He wondered if the door had been white once.

The Inspector opened the door and stood to one side. "In!"

The junior officer pushed hard again and Charlie had to thrust his hands out to stop smashing into the wall.

"Sit!" The Inspector thwatted the table with his cane.

Charlie was re-cuffed, hands behind his back, pushed down and then locked to the chair. He wanted to yell at the top of his voice, "It isn't mine; it isn't mine!" But he could not because half the bust *was* his. He recited Grover's name in his head, a mantra, "You bastard, you fucking bastard."

Inspector Fernandez pulled out a cigarette and took his time to light it. The puff billowed, "Yes, Mr Carter, you have been extremely foolish."

∞

Yesterday.

Charlie ordered another beer and a plate of chips called French Fries. Sazoras was as good a place as any to relax during the heat of the day. He watched some fishermen unload their catch and drag an ancient timber fishing boat up the beach on logs used as rollers. They sang and talked loudly as the catch was distributed. Local children played and swam in the shallows. Dogs and black raven seabirds manoeuvred for position nearby, hoping for some luck with the left-overs.

He smiled, noting some local lads trying their luck with some northern European girls in bikinis. It said in the guidebook for female foreigners to dress modestly so as not to offend the locals. It was clear to him that these young men were not offended in the slightest as they asked to have their picture taken with the beautiful young Nords.

Charlie peeled through some of the magazines lying on the table, had another beer and then returned to the Steep Beach. He was not sure about swimming at the main beach. Floating debris took the shine off it. The hotel had a good swimming pool, although it warmed up a little during the day. He was also more than keen to put a smoke together and try the new stuff.

That night, Charlie joined some Brits clubbing at the Silver Balloon. It was crowded, hot and humid, just the weather for drinking. The loud thump of house music and yelling young people signalled the use of artificial stimulants. He managed to crank up a conversation with some Israeli girls who had just completed military service. He managed to remember a few names. A group of them were staying at the next beach, Calangute. Some of the tables on the wooden floor seemed to move with the music, so Charlie made his way to the mosaic tiled area and had a few more drinks. Several hours later, in the early morning, he was sitting at the tables on the sand. The music was still loud, and several joints made their way around.

He hooligan-ed his way home with the Brits as first light flicked and glinted through the rice fields. Charlie passed out in a deep sleep to the clicking of the fan and the thump of house music buried in his head.

∞

Today.

A dog barked somewhere out in the compound beyond a barred window.

He knew he had to say something. "Sir, that marijuana is not mine."

Inspector Fernandez took another drag on his cigarette and blew a spout to the side. "It was found in your possession Mr. Carter." The dark marble eyes did not leave Charlie's face.

"Look, I don't know how it got there. Someone must have put it there." Sweat trickled down his face. He could not do anything other than shake his head with hands tied behind. All the time he could feel the heat of the junior officer behind.

"I see. And what about the hashish? I suppose that's not yours either?"

The Inspector rattled something to the junior officer who turned the fan on and went out leaving the door ajar. The fan squeaked and turned, as if on a camshaft.

"Mr Carter, we get all sorts of people coming here to Goa flouting our rules and regulations. You have been charged with possession of a dangerous drug, a very serious charge."

He stood, butted out the cigarette in a metal ashtray and walked out.

The cuffs dug into his wrists and his shoulders cramped. Now Charlie was on his own he should have felt calmer, but confusion and fear of the future made his heart thump. He tried to deep breathe. Looking around the room did not help. The walls of the grubby cream room were decorated with dents, scratches, and ugly, grey plaster. There were small spots of crimson here and there at head height. He knew they were different from the bright red beetle juice stains down low in the corner.

Charlie tried to scroll the things in his head. He was less sure now that Grover was behind it. Only a small thing; Grover said he did not deal in marijuana. Could the cops have organised it all without Grover knowing? Hard to believe. The bloke at the front desk at the Steep Beach seemed a bit strange. Could have been him. Maybe one of the staff had observed him blowing a joint near the pool? Maybe Rodriguez was not cool; maybe the money changer or someone nearby saw the wad of notes in his bum-bag, maybe one of the boys at Sazoras? Maybe it was just one of those things.

The door swung open. "Now, Mr Carter, what are we to do with you?" He sat down and looked hard at Charlie.

"Inspector … I would like to speak to a lawyer."

The Inspector leaned back in the chair and chuckled, more of a smirk. "Mr Carter, you have been watching too much television." The borderline mirth disappeared in a click. "This is not America, not Australia also. You get a lawyer only if we decide you can have one."

"Who dobbed … who gave you this information on me?"

The Inspector whacked the table with his cane. Charlie jumped. "I am not at liberty to discuss matters such as that."

"But sir, that marijuana is not mine. I'll..l … I admit that the hash is mine. But the marijuana is not mine."

"Who are you suggesting put it there then? I do hope you are not suggesting that we did, Mr Carter?"

"No, of course not. But someone did. That marijuana is not mine." Charlie hoped that the policeman had not picked up on the desperation in his statement.

The Inspector stood again and walked out. The dog outside in the compound started barking again. Charlie stared at the open door, aware of the suppressed violence, abuse, corruption and possibly even justice taking place outside. He did not have the opportunity to focus. The junior officer marched in. Charlie cringed, ready for the bashing.

The man slipped behind, undid his cuffs, and stood aside. "You follow."

Charlie let out a long breath and pushed himself up onto his jelly legs.

They went towards the front of the building through a large room with desks, phones, and officials. A door loomed. The junior officer knocked, opened the door, and nudged Charlie in, then stepped out and closed the door. Inspector Fernandez, arms folded, leaned against a table. His cane was jammed under his arm.

"Mr Carter, I have given this case much consideration and I have decided to release you. There are conditions, of course."

Charlie rubbed his bruised wrists. "Conditions?" He was not sure if he was dizzy or dreaming.

"You will be formally charged for the hashish and released on a good behaviour bond. The matter of the marijuana is still a serious issue. I am prepared to overlook that if you leave Goa as soon as practicable"

Charlie's heart thumped and his lower stomach puckered.

"Sign this." The Inspector handed him a pen and pointed to a sheet of paper on the grubby table.

Charlie picked up the paper. It was difficult to read, his hands quaked. Fortunately, it was written in English.

"Mr Carter, I have offered you the opportunity to walk out of here free. All you are doing by signing that document is agreeing to the charges of possession of hashish."

Charlie scanned the page again and signed at the bottom. He hoped it was not noticed that the signature was not identical to his passport. He had not intended it that way but his hand shook and the table was rough underneath.

"Here are your possessions, Mr Carter." The Inspector tipped the contents of the cloth bag onto the scratched deal table and flicked the passport on top.

Charlie grabbed the passport, bum-bag, and wallet.

"I will show you out."

The Inspector marched out. They went through a hot, noisy room full of rank and file. Charlie could feel the despair and depression as he stumbled behind. The imposing junior officer was leaning against a concrete pillar with his big brown arms folded. Charlie could see the nasty smile on his face, so he tried to focus on the red squirts of beetle juice in the corners of the steps. They reached the bottom.

Inspector Fernandez pointed his cane, "You will find a taxi just down the road. Remember the conditions Mr Carter. You are to leave Goa within the next two days and if you have any sense, you will never come back here."

Charlie stood for a second then walked past the surly gate officer and down the road. His legs felt like rubber but he had to maintain what little dignity was left. He knew those marble eyes were on him.

He turned the corner and sat down on a stone wall bordering a pile of refuse. People stared and gave him a wide berth, considering him too damaged to offer special prices. The late afternoon sun sliced through the coconut palms hurting his head and his insides felt about to give way. He forced himself to take deep yoga breaths and it took all his control to not cry. A mangy dog came over, looked at him and then sat down in sympathy nearby. After a time, he did not know how long, he looked in the bum-bag. The twenty-eight hundred Australian dollars were gone. He fiddled in his wallet with clumsy fingers. Sweat dripped off his forehead. The credit cards were still there. The bastards had left him just enough rupees to get a taxi back to the Steep Beach Hotel.

Charlie stood up, still wonky. As he walked, a feeling of strength slowly crept over him. Strangely, he now felt ready to deal with any minor problems awaiting him in Australia.

The end

Every action has consequences

Contracts must be honoured

The correct choice is critical

WATERPIPE

"Useless prick of a thing," grumbled Garth.

The supermarket trolley rhomboided with a mind of its own across the tar-and-puddle car park. His stomach muscles twisted and strained trying to keep the *Bastards Incorporated* contraption heading in the right direction.

Garth should have been happier because the recalcitrant trolley had the potential to take his mind off his money worries. *The fucking landlord, the bank, the ex-missus. And the dole office - he did not get his form in on time so they cut off his money. Bastards, kick a bloke in the guts when he's down, they don't know what it's like to struggle!* He needed a hit of heroin.

The lacy drizzle gently fizzed from the gravel-grey sky all the time he was in the shopping centre and was not about to let up now. He juggled the car keys out of his pocket and pressed the remote.

"Eh?"

The lights flashed on his car *and* the BMW parked alongside. He did it again with the same result.

"What the ...?"

The trolley still tugged at his stomach muscles, like a Rottweiler on a lead who had just spied a Chihuahua. His rusty Camry's back bumper stopped the rolling cage. Clunk.

"I'll be rooted," he muttered and pressed the remote again.

Both vehicles unlocked. He opened the Camry boot; glancing casually around as he transferred his shopping bags. The car park was about quarter full, no one was particularly looking at him.

Garth opened the passenger door of the Beemer. *That new smell, only new cars smelled like that, rich bastards.* The console between the seats revealed bugger all. Tissues, a box of frangers, a couple of CDs, a comb and half a packet of mints.

"Bugger," he grumbled and checked the glove box. "Fuck."

He stepped back and straightened up, gently closing the door as he glanced around. About twenty metres away a young mother, with generous hips and half-moon shapes of bum jellying out each side of her tight shorts, tried to subdue a bawling child in a pram and at the same time load her rust bucket with shopping bags.

Garth tossed the rest of his shopping in his boot and had to lean on it a couple of times to click it closed. A quick glance around, no worries. His peripheral vision registered a plastic bag trying to defy gravity. In the damp, lacy rain it chased a piece of paper across the car park through the grit. The evening darkness waited, ready to come in.

He opened the rear door of the BMW. It had the same money feel - Garth knew all about those sorts of people. He rifled through a heap of stuff on the floor. A jumper, several magazines, a half empty water bottle, a purple, furry apple core and a red folder half pushed under the seat. He unzipped it.

"Aha!" A glow and a smile cracked his encroaching five o'clock shadow. "Christ Almighty, buried treasure!"

His shaking hands fingered piles of notes clipped together, used, and new, all denominations as far as a quick peek could tell. Garth flashed a glance at the dashboard in case he'd missed something. Nothing there, neat, and tidy. Only a small soccer ball clipped to the rear vision mirror.

He knew he had to be quick. It was difficult to step back on weak legs. The BMW door clicked and he threw the folder into his car. No time to roll a cigarette, his hands shaky. He hit the starter and slowly drove towards the exit. The battling mother was trying to strap the mini, screaming windmill into a baby seat. Garth had trouble taking his eyes off the shapely bum bursting out of her shorts. Cold, oily winter sun glinted off the puddles, a confirmation of the gritty stamp of winter. If there was time he would have sat and watched her but there were other more important things to do.

He felt as if a god from somewhere had given him a chance, shown him the up on the rungs, lit a bright star in his life. Maybe his luck was changing at last. No-one deserved it more than him.

His hands slipped on the steering wheel and concentration became difficult. In the next street he had to get out to close the boot that had popped up as he drove along. When he jumped back in the driver's seat the urge was too strong, he had to fiddle with the money again. A quick estimate, at least five thousand dollars. Nervous eyes reflected off the rear vision mirror. No one paid any attention to him, nothing out of the ordinary. No worries there.

∞

He drove around a bit to be doubly sure, past the industrial area of landfill producing warehouses and into suburbs. The late afternoon sun hid behind charcoal-cotton clouds trying to drag down the dying day. He lit a butt from the ashtray, desperate to have a smoke. A smile tickled the edges of his dry mouth as he sped home, eager to make a call. The Camry lurched to a stop on the lawn of weeds and started rolling again as he was half out. He hit *park*. Keys jumbled with his fingers, but the front door eventually creaked open.

He grabbed the phone. "Come on, come on, dick brain."

The Man picked up. "Yeah?"

Through code Garth established there was some good quality heroin in stock. "No worries, mate," he said. "See ya soon."

∞

He tipped the contents of the folder onto the kitchen table. Apart from the notes there was expensive, watermark writing paper and an equally expensive, gold-nibbed Parker fountain pen.

"Always wanted a fountain pen," he mumbled as he fumbled out a tailor-made cigarette from a crushed pack lying near the phone. Fingers flickered like the lighter; no way could he put a rollie together yet.

He was too excited about scoring heroin to count the money accurately, but he stopped at four thousand with the bigger notes. There was at least another thousand in smaller notes. "Fucking beauty!" he yelped grabbing the car keys.

The visit with *The Man* was fruitful as he was able to score some quality marijuana in addition to the heroin. He needed to call in at the shady, *Sweet and Juicy's* chemist shop, near the market to buy some more needles. SJ's was really Swzettenzjswzi. No one could say it, let alone spell it, but all the junkies knew it was the place to get needles, no questions asked.

The Man never let Garth, or any of his other customers, inject at his place because he claimed he did not have any spare needles. In reality, he did not want the potential problems associated with a user overdosing in his lounge room. It was his business and he was not a health care worker.

Garth only had one needle at home and after sharpening it on emery paper the last few times, injecting heroin made ugly purple dots up his arm. The chemist, SJ, looked at him through glassy, bombed out eyes and smiled. Garth nodded and took off through the oily streets and in his haste almost knocked over the other gate post when he arrived home. He stumbled past the rotting mattress on the overgrown lawn that the landlord always complained about. A gang of crows tried to pull rank on each other at the overturned rubbish bin on the footpath. They bullied and harassed as darkness descended.

∞

For the next few days Garth injected regularly, seeking new spots to ease in the dangerous, but so rewarding, hypodermic wire. He smoked numerous joints and watched television. It was ecstasy to have piles of money, smack, and puff. He rang his ex-wife and told her to back off with the cops because he had some money coming for her and the kids. She was hyper on slimming tablets and easy to handle, always eager to take dollars from him. His only outing was to the corner shop to get a jar of coffee, milk, packets of tobacco, a carton of Marlborough and a box of cigarette papers. Three days later he got the call. He and *The Man* were going into business.

He said, "How's it going, mate? Let's talk, eh?"

∞

Next morning, Garth rolled off the dog's bed lounge onto the floor out of delirium sleep. He thought there was a knock on the door. Pre-withdrawals mauled his head. The knock came again.

"All right, you greedy fucking bitch," he grumbled.

He should have realised his wife would have come around like this. Garth opened the door and tried to focus.

A well-dressed, middle-aged bald man smiled. "Sir, are you Mr Garth Pringle?"

Garth was not together enough to think anything before responding.

"Er … um … yeah, maybe, who wants to know?" He clutched the door jamb trying to be in control of things. A wave of nausea sweat prickled his forehead.

The other man ran a scarred hand over his bald head as if he had hair. He had gold rings on two fingers. The little finger was missing. He stuck his other hand out in greeting, ignoring Garth's comment about who wants to know.

Seemed friendly enough. Garth was still not thinking clearly and drooped his hand half out. The other man grabbed to shake it and with moray speed, whipped out a piece of water pipe from behind his back. *Whack!* Garth's wrist splintered. As quick as that! A muted animal yelp burst from his mouth and he slid down the door jamb.

"Mr Pringle, you borrowed six thousand, seven hundred and seventy-five dollars from my client."

He looked away towards the park. A boy and a dog played in the distance. His bald head swivelled back. The glare returned, hard and serious. The scarred hand with showy rings went up like a gentle stop sign.

"Now, my client Mister, let's call him Mister X, is a very understanding sort of gentleman. He realises people have money problems from time to time, and also, sometimes, people borrow things from other people from time to time."

Garth did not care about the tears trickling down his face. He looked up dazed, trying to contain the pain. Vomit threatened to explode out of him. He held his smashed right wrist, blood trickled through his fingers.

"Of course, in these instances there are always costs that need to be added to the principal and Mister X has generously settled on a figure of fifteen thousand dollars. You are very lucky to catch him in a charitable mood; there was talk of twenty thousand. The term of the repayment contract is cash, naturally, and that is due seven working days from now."

Garth's eyes glistened with the tears of fear, pain and lack of understanding and he still could not speak. His weak sobs punctuated the cold morning. Several drops of blood rallied to form a pool on the cracked concrete verandah at his feet.

"You shouldn't have looked at the soccer ball, the roving eye camera on the rear vision mirror, sir. You also should have latched your boot properly too, because a helpful young woman remembered you and tried to wave you down. Aaah, the public are always so helpful, Mr Pringle." Bald man's eyebrows did an opening drawbridge.

Garth now looked up from his shattered wrist and the shaking had nothing to do with the cold.

"Right, Mr Pringle, one week, I'll contact you and if you think you might pull a fast one, think again. The foundations of Mister X's high-rise buildings contain many a fool who thought he could get away without honouring a contract. Fifteen thousand dollars in used notes. One week. Understand?"

Garth started to move his head very slowly up and down like a tired cow at the abattoir.

"I didn't get that. What did you say?" The bald man fluttered the damaged hand slowly over his head again. The rings glistened in reflected light from the front window.

Garth tried again. "Yyyeah …" Snot and tears mingled around his mouth.

"Great stuff, Mr Pringle. Pleasure to do business with you, sir. Oh, by the way, my name is Mister Y, I'm a debt collector. See you later. *Mate*."

Garth sat slumped in the doorway. Two minutes later his eyes focussed. A car pulled up. His wife jumped out, followed by her boyfriend.

The end.

Skirting the truth –

Sometimes gets results

Is there a price to pay?

LIES

"Sorry, sir, the gate is closed."

"The taxi was late, and there were roadworks."

Slight glare. "I'm sorry sir; we have rules we have to adhere to."

"But, but it's only a minute late."

"I'm sorry, but really it's five minutes late."

"Oh, is it? Sorry my watch must be wrong. I get mixed up with the daylight-saving times." He tries a gooey smile.

The flight attendant official sighs. "I'm sorry sir, the gate is closed. You will have to re-book over there." She points to an unstaffed counter, turns to her computer, and starts tapping away. Conversation over.

Elmore tries again, it is worth a go. "Look, please, I just had a serious operation on my shoulder and I would have great difficulty going back into town and finding accommodation. And also, I didn't really want to mention this, but my mother is really ill ... and she is elderly, she's in hospital and she might ..."

"Rachel?" Standing nearby, sympathetic middle-aged Flight Attendant Supervisor, Helen, straightening the plastic name tag on her generous chest, intervenes. "He's just got a shoulder bag and the small crew bag. I think we can make an exception on this occasion, provided he hurries."

Rachel scowls at Helen and then eyeballs Elmore. "Mmm. Okay sir; please put your bag up here."

Elmore makes a big thing of his fictitious shoulder injury with the bag manoeuvre.

Rachel, darkening aura, verbally stabs, "Gate 25." She has great difficulty saying, "*please,* and you will need to hurry."

Helen, quickly examining his ticket adds, "Maybe you can organise his baggage to go on board? To save him dragging the crew bag, with that bad shoulder, you know, through security and to the gate?" She smiles at Elmore and moves away.

Rachel sneers after her departing supervisor and turns. "I bet that business about your shoulder is a lot of bull and your mother? *Christ.*" She rolls her eyes and barks into her walkie-talkie.

He winks at her and says, "You're a champ."

Her face is now grey but under control, "Gate 25."

She hands the bag to a man in overalls. Elmore takes off towards security, rubbing his right shoulder and smiling. Speakers bellow and screech flight details at the shiny surfaces of the terminal. A group of five female Nordic backpackers time their assault on security one second in front of Elmore. He tries to get around them.

"Hey bud, wait your turn, these people got here before you," yells a security man.

Elmore reckoned the mongrel has the aptitude to be a future senior parking inspector. The only thing missing is the Gestapo badge on his uniform. "Cock-head," he mutters and aloud he says, "Mate, my flight, AF887 is just about to take off."

"Ya shoulda thought of that before, buddy." Gestapo Bud had moved his gaze from the breasts to eyeing off the girls' tanned legs that seemed to keep going up for ever.

Elmore had to get moving. "But mate ... I've only got a wallet, that's all, no other stuff. My flight is just about to take off."

Gestapo Bud holds up his hand, not taking his eyes off the girl's bra-less chests under their T-shirts. "Wait your turn."

Sweat drips in Elmore's eyes as he glances at his watch and finally, he makes his way through security, but then ...

"Sir, will you please step this way. Are you carrying any explosives?" A stick-thin, Botox-lipped, safety-pin through the nose woman in uniform, waves a wand. Elmore knows she is not a fairy princess. *Shit a brick.*

"What? Does it look like I …? Quick, my flight … never mind." He knows it is pointless to even react.

"Sorry to delay you," clearly not sorry, "I'm just doing my job," dribbles the Goth, "please raise your arms." She waves the wand over him.

Elmore takes off at a brisk pace for Gate 25. Sweat drips down his back, his underwear chafes.

Gate 22 coming up. A group of Asians, obviously on tour, dawdle and chatter excitedly, and he uses up valuable time getting through their remonstrating arms and ridiculous amount of cabin baggage and gimmicks. His shoulder feels very sore.

Gate 23. He is still dodging around people who have no concept of social conscience or consideration of others, let alone doing the right thing. A family, obviously a family, stretches six abreast, unconsciously making sure no one else can get through. Dad, wearing Flatfoot the Clown thongs, a T-shirt ready for the op shop with *Gobble me* on the front, a verandah gut over balloon shorts, frowns at his wife who is trying to control four over excited kids in need of a bath.

"Hey, steady on mate, where's the fire?" quips dad.

Elmore ignores the comment, he seems to be on jelly legs. Past Gate 24. The pain in his shoulder is worse. He notices that it is now the left shoulder. And his neck. He arrives at Gate 25 his heart is pounding, and his ears feel funny. His head feels cold and hot at the same time, must be the sweat and the air-conditioning.

An announcement blasts out, so loud it makes him jump. "We apologise for the delay of flight number AF887. You will be boarding in about 10 minutes after flight AF 663 has completed disembarking."

He sees through translucence, people marching *into* the terminal through Gate 25. *Bugger!* They have not even unloaded. The pain has moved down from his shoulder, to his chest, on the left-hand side. His temples pulse as if they are going to burst. The pain in behind his ribs is acute. He feels weak and dizzy.

Elmore grabs at his chest and crumples to the ground, gasping. Someone yells for help.

The end

Acknowledgements

Writing is a challenging, frustrating, joyous, satisfying pursuit and my interactions with other writers and readers along the way has been enormously helpful.

I would like to thank the following people (in alphabetical order) for their support and feedback in my early writing days when I wrote the original version of some of these stories: Ian Austin, Bronwyn Cozens, Michael Doneman, Pam Hardgrave, Laurie Keim, Rosemary Laver, Denise Miller, Tess McLeod, Andrea Rankin, and Steve Reilly.

Special acknowledgement to two fine ladies, now deceased, who always encouraged and supported my writing endeavours: Beryl Corris and Beryl Muspratt.

Thanks also to my friends at the Coolum Wave Writers, Sunshine Coast Literary Association, and the Queensland Writers Centre.

The front cover of this book is a photograph of the sun setting in Goa, India and it is connected to the story, *Price of Liberty*. Thanks to Morgana (Tess) McLeod for her assistance in the initial phase of designing this cover. Many thanks once again to Jan Forbes for her design work on the final cover.

As always, special thanks to my family for believing in me.

About the Author

Ian Laver, a well-travelled fiction writer living in south east Queensland, has written and published two novels, CRUCIAL STEP and UNEASY. He has written several collections of short stories, and many of his stories have been published in anthologies and magazines. DEADLY SINS contains a varied selection of his short stories.

Ian was editor of a small country association magazine and had a regular column in an online publication. He was President of the Sunshine Coast Literary Association, has been active in writing organisations and is at present involved in Haiku and creative writing groups. Two Henry Lawson Emerging Writer prizes and a Tom Howard Short Story Award are listed among his more than a dozen writing awards.

You can discover more about Ian's writing at-
Facebook: https://www.facebook.com/ian.laver.18
Facebook author page: Ian Laver | Facebook
Website: https://www.ianlaver.net
Instagram: https://www.instagram.com/iwlaver/